B40 1/14

Because of Shoe

AND OTHER DOG STORIES

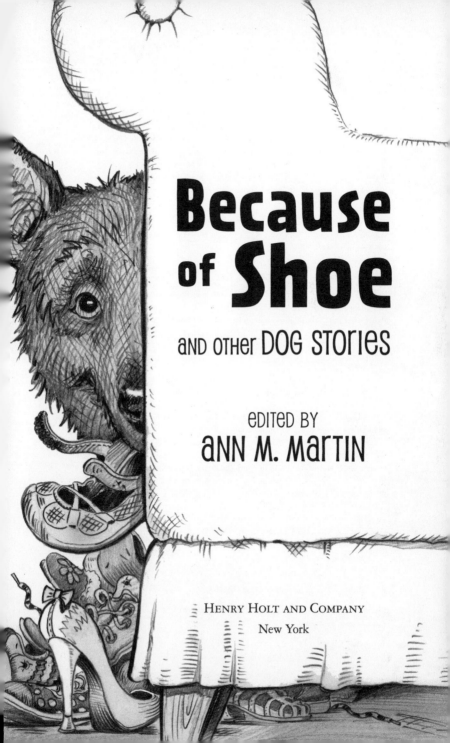

Because of Shoe

AND OTHER DOG STORIES

EDITED BY
ANN M. MARTIN

HENRY HOLT AND COMPANY
New York

Permission to reproduce the following is gratefully acknowledged: "Things People Can't See" © 2012 by Matt de la Peña; "Trail Magic" © 2012 by Margarita Engle; "The God of the Pond" © 2012 by Valerie Hobbs; "Patty" (text and illustrations) © 2012 by Thacher Hurd; "Picasso" © 2012 by Ann M. Martin; "Because of Shoe" © 2012 by Pam Muñoz Ryan; "Brancusi & Me" (text and illustrations) © 2012 by Jon J Muth; "Dognapper" © 2012 by Wendy Orr; "Science Fair" (text and illustrations) © 2012 by Mark Teague.

Henry Holt and Company, LLC
Publishers since 1866
175 Fifth Avenue
New York, New York 10010
mackids.com

Library of Congress Cataloging-in-Publication Data
    Because of Shoe and other dog stories / edited by Ann M. Martin.—1st ed.
    v.   cm.
    Summary: An illustrated anthology of stories about dogs and their
relationships with humans, for readers of varying levels.
    Contents: Dognapper / by Wendy Orr — Because of Shoe / by Pam Muñoz Ryan — Science fair / by Mark Teague — Patty / by Thacher Hurd — Picasso / by Ann M. Martin — The God of the Pond / by Valerie Hobbs — Trail magic / by Margarita Engle — Things people can't see / by Matt de la Peña — Brancusi & me / by Jon J. Muth.
    ISBN 978-0-8050-9314-8 (hc)
    1. Dogs—Juvenile fiction.   2. Children's stories, American.   [1. Dogs—Fiction.   2. Short stories.]   I. Martin, Ann M.
    PZ5.B388 2012
    [Fic]—dc23

                                                                    2011033501

First Edition—2012 / Designed by Elynn Cohen

Printed in the United States of America by R. R. Donnelley & Sons Company, Harrisonburg, Virginia

10 9 8 7 6 5 4 3 2 1

Contents

Editor's Note

SADIE

Bonjour. *Je m'appelle* Sadie Martin. I am Ann Martin's dog, and I don't really speak French, but like some of the dogs you'll read about in this collection of stories, I enjoy showing off occasionally.

Also, not to brag, but if it weren't for me, you wouldn't be reading this collection at all. For most of her life, Ann Martin was a cat person.

Then, when she was forty-two years old, she adopted me, her first dog. By the time I was housebroken and had learned a few commands, Ann had fallen in love with me. Therefore, I was solely responsible for turning her from a cat person into a dog-and-cat person. And this is why, when someone at Henry Holt and Company, the publisher of this book, asked Ann if she'd like to edit a collection of stories about dogs, her answer was yes.

At this point, you're probably saying, "Thank you for all your good work, Sadie!"

You're welcome.

Between the covers of this book you'll read about a boy who turns into a dog, a dog who brings a family together, a dog who lived a long time ago and was a companion to a very great artist in Paris, and about funny dogs, adventurous dogs, brave dogs, smart dogs, and dogs who perform rescues. I'm happy to have been able to bring you this collection of stories, and I hope you enjoy reading about the superior race of canines.

—Sadie Martin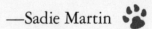

Dognapper

by Wendy Orr

illustrated by Olga and Aleksey Ivanov

Max

Tyler could hear Max howling as soon as he turned onto his street.

Max the Dax never howled, except when Tyler's mom, Officer Olson, drove up the driveway with her police siren on—she liked doing that when she finished work the same time as Tyler finished school. But school had let out early today because of the Grand Parade.

The parade that opened the county fair was the biggest event of the year. There would be brass bands, firefighters and police, jugglers, popcorn sellers, baton twirlers, fancy horses, and performing dogs. Tyler's mom would be marching with the other police officers—but the parade didn't start for two more hours. Right now she was still at work, and there was no siren to be heard.

If Max was howling, then something was wrong.

Tyler started to run.

Max was a black weiner dog with tan bits on his chest like a bikini top, twitchy tan eyebrows, and a tan nose. His legs were short and stumpy, his back was long, and his bark was as deep and strong as the bark of Officer Olson's police dog, Gus.

Gus was a German shepherd; he was very smart and very well trained. Tyler's mom said he knew more about right and wrong than most people did. Sometimes he stole bones from Max and dropped them over the front fence, to remind Max that he was bigger and stronger, but Tyler's mom said he was just teasing.

Gus

Lately Gus had been much too busy to tease Max. He was the only police dog in town, and two weeks ago the poodlenappings had begun.

Cassandra Caniche's silver poodle was the first to disappear. Cassandra herself was as elegant and graceful as any prizewinning poodle. She ran the Poodle Parlor, and when she'd washed and cut her poodle customers' wool, she spun and wove it into wonderful capes and coats.

But now every poodle that had been groomed at Cassandra's parlor had disappeared. Tyler's mom and Gus had searched everywhere, but they hadn't found a single clue.

By the day of the parade, eleven poodles were missing.

Tyler grabbed the emergency key from under a rock. He was supposed to go next door to tell Mrs. Lacey he was home before he picked up Max, but he couldn't wait to find out what was wrong with his dog. His hands were sweating as he unlocked the door and tapped in the security code.

Max stopped howling when he saw Tyler, but he whined restlessly at the front door, hackles prickling and brown eyes anxious. He didn't even ask for a pat.

Something was badly wrong.

Tyler grabbed his phone. He had just pressed "Mom" when Mrs. Lacey pounded at the front door.

"Have you got Pippa?" she gasped.

Pippa the poodle was Max's very best dog friend. She had creamy curls and long dark eyelashes. If she and Max hadn't played together for a few days, Pippa would bounce up and down in her yard, her silky ears flapping high over the fence, until Max started digging. Max had short stubby legs, but his shoulders were strong, and his paws were nearly as big as Gus's. When he dug a tunnel from his yard to Pippa's, dirt sprayed so far out behind him it disappeared like magic.

Pippa

Now it was Pippa who had disappeared like magic.

Pippa had been poodlenapped.

"Tyler?" said his mom's voice.

"Max!" shouted Tyler, and tossed the phone to Mrs. Lacey as the dachshund slipped between his legs.

The little dog raced across the lawn to Mrs. Lacey's back gate. He was whining so pitifully that Tyler let him in so that he could see for himself that Pippa was gone.

Max ran straight up to the back door. A chunk of raw steak was on the top step, and the dachshund gulped it down before Tyler could stop him.

"That's strange!" thought Tyler. Mrs. Lacey always cooked Pippa's dinner and fed her in the kitchen.

Max checked the steps for more food and lolloped through the open dog door.

"Even stranger!" thought Tyler. Pippa's dog door had been locked tight since the first poodlenapping.

But the flap had been unscrewed from the outside—and a scrap of navy blue fabric was caught in the corner of the dog door.

Mrs. Lacey, when she wasn't wearing a creamy Pippa-wool coat that Cassandra had woven, wore mostly pink. She hated navy blue because, when she was six, she'd fallen out of a boat while she was wearing her brand-new sailor suit. She'd never worn that color again.

Tyler pulled the scrap out and put it in his pocket.

He called Max, and the dachshund's nose appeared through the door. His head and front legs followed, and finally his back legs and tail. He slinked down the steps and scratched at the gate to the carport.

Mrs. Lacey opened the door. "Come in," she said, sniffing sadly. "Your mom's on her way."

Tyler followed her back into her house. Mrs. Lacey plunked down at her kitchen table and burst into tears. "All the time I was out shopping, I was thinking about the fun we'd have going to the parade to watch your mom and Gus. Then I opened the door, ready for Pippa to jump up the way she does, with her front paws around my neck . . . but she wasn't here!"

Tyler didn't know what to do. Seeing Mrs. Lacey cry was almost as bad as wondering where Pippa was. He gave her a box of tissues and a hug, just like she used to do for him when he was little. Then he fixed her a cup of coffee. That made her smile, but she still couldn't stop crying.

"Mom and Gus will find Pippa," Tyler reassured her, and looked outside to see if they were coming.

The yard was empty, front and back.

Max was gone too.

A cold hand of fear closed tight around Tyler's neck, but as he jumped off the back steps, the fear burst into a fiery rage. No one was going to steal his dog!

Then he saw the tunnel. Max hadn't been stolen—he'd dug under the fence and escaped through the carport. Tyler raced down the driveway, but there was no sign of a short-legged, long black dog.

Tyler started to run.

Max was tracking.

Max had always been a pet, but his great-great-great-grandparents had been hunting dogs, and Max's nose was a sniffing, tracking, hunting nose. That nose followed the scent of Pippa and the poodlenapper out to the carport and locked on to the smell of the vehicle they'd driven away in.

Being a small dog who lives with a police dog is a bit like being a little boy with a grown-up brother—sometimes Max wished he could go to work every day doing exciting things, instead of staying home all alone, waiting for Tyler to get home from school. But right now he wasn't thinking about Gus, or Tyler, or anything at all except following that scent.

Luckily the dognapper had taken quiet back streets. Max was running along the scent trail of the tire closest to the sidewalk, but it was still a precarious place for a small dog.

Tyler ran as fast as he could to where their street met a busy road. It was a good plan, because that would have been the most dangerous way of all for Max to go.

It was a good plan, except that it wasn't the way Max had gone.

Tyler turned down the busy road and kept on running until he heard a police siren.

People on the road stared as a police car,

with a large German shepherd in the back, pulled up beside the boy. Tyler didn't notice the stares. He jumped into the back seat beside Gus.

"Max has gone too!" he gasped. "I think he's following the dognapper."

"He's not a trained tracker," said his mom. "He could be anywhere!"

She cruised slowly down the street for a mile and then turned around. "He couldn't have gotten farther than this. We'll go back to Mrs. Lacey's and let Gus start tracking properly."

Mrs. Lacey had been so shocked when Max disappeared too that she knew she had to do something. By the time Tyler and his mom returned, she was knocking on the door across the road, asking if they'd seen anyone go to her house that morning or seen Max run away half an hour ago.

She'd been to three houses already, and no one had seen anything.

"Only the parcel delivery van," said one neighbor.

"I haven't ordered anything!" Mrs. Lacey exclaimed.

"Well, that's what I thought it was," said the neighbor. "It was a white van—or maybe cream. Actually, I think it was light brown."

"That's very helpful," said Officer Olson, who had joined Mrs. Lacey and was jotting everything down in a notebook.

Mrs. Lacey and Tyler showed his mom Pippa's open dog door and Max's tunnel from the backyard to the carport.

"Seek!" Tyler's mom ordered.

Gus sniffed at the tunnel, then trotted along the driveway and down the road, away from the busy street Tyler had run to.

"I'll go on asking the neighbors," said Mrs. Lacey. She started for the next house.

Tyler jogged after Gus. He couldn't help thinking that if he'd turned that way the first time, he might have found Max already.

His mom cruised slowly behind in the

police car, following Tyler, who was jogging after Gus, who was tracking Max, who was hunting the poodlenapper who'd stolen Pippa.

Max was still running along the side of the road with his nose to the ground. He was tracking so hard, he hadn't noticed how sore his paws were or how thirsty he was, but his legs were moving more slowly and he was panting heavily.

The street had turned into a country road. The houses were big, with wide lawns and tall fences. There were exciting country smells of horses, sheep, other dogs, rabbits, and squirrels. Max would have loved to stop and sniff if he hadn't been so busy tracking Pippa.

Then the scent led Max up the driveway to a building humming with hair dryers. Chemical shampoo smells wafted out, drowning everything else, and Max had to circle for a moment before he found Pippa's own poodley, best-friend scent again. He followed it out of the driveway and on down the road.

Half a mile along was a huge old house, with the widest lawns and tallest fences of all. It had black chimneys, tiny windows, and pointy Rapunzel towers. The fence and gates were black iron with sharp spears on top; the bars were so close together that Max had to put his nose right up to them to see through.

But Max wasn't staring. He was sniffing, and even though he couldn't see them, he could smell dogs. Lots of dogs. And somewhere in that rich bouquet of dog scents, he could smell Pippa.

Max bayed his big, deep bark, and from a hidden pen behind the house, he heard Pippa's shrill yip.

Max started to dig.

Tyler was in the police car with his mom. He was getting more and more worried. If he'd become too tired to run any farther, how could Max still be tracking, on his six-inch-long legs? Even Gus was starting to look tired.

Then Gus circled in a hairdresser's driveway. Officer Olson parked the car and went inside.

Excitement and fear spidered up Tyler's throat. Any second now, his mom was going to find his dog and maybe Pippa too. But what if the dognapper was still in there?

His mother came back out just as Gus found the scent again. "No one there has seen a dog all day," she said.

Inside the dark house, a man was throwing a torn navy blue shirt into his trash can when he heard a deep bark.

He shuddered. He was sure it was the same police dog he'd heard that morning, from the house next door to the beautiful poodle. It had made him shake so badly, he'd nearly dropped her as he ran to the van.

Now the big-voiced dog was at his gates. He needed to get out of there fast, before it brought the police to his door.

The van was still backed up against the poodle pen. Two minutes later, it was tearing down the driveway.

The fence was set deep in the ground, and Max was head down, with dirt spraying out behind him. He was digging too hard to hear the electric gates swish open.

He did hear the skid of gravel as the van sped onto the road—but once Max was digging, he couldn't stop. The heavy gates clanged shut, and he dug even faster.

From inside the speeding police car, Tyler stared at the huge old house with the black iron fence and gates. A cloud of dirt was spraying out from under the fence. In the middle of the cloud of dirt, he could see the tip of a long black tail.

"Max!" Tyler screamed, and his mother slammed on the brakes.

Max slithered out of the tunnel and into the garden. He sniffed the air and knew Pippa had gone. He turned around and crawled back under the fence to Tyler.

Tyler hugged him. So did his mom. She checked that the little dog wasn't hurt and lifted him into the back seat.

"You've gotten us this far, Max!" she said as they jumped back into the car. "Now let's finish the job!" She spoke into her police radio and took off after the disappearing cloud of dust.

The siren screamed; the light flashed; houses and lawns blurred past. Tyler sat tight, holding Max. He'd never been with his mom when she was chasing a bad guy. He'd never gone anywhere so fast!

But the van was too far ahead. They were still two blocks behind when they reached the town. They could see the van turn onto Main Street.

By the time they got there, it had disappeared.

"We'll never catch him now!" exclaimed Tyler. There was so much traffic, they couldn't see ahead—and there were so many side streets and alleys that they could never guess which one the van might have turned down.

The police radio crackled. Tyler couldn't hear what the officer on the other end was saying, but it made his mom smile.

"There's something the dognapper doesn't know about Main Street today," she said as the police car inched along through the traffic and the crowds thronging both sides of the street. "All the side roads are blocked off. The road we just came in on was closed as soon as we turned off it—there's only one way the van can go."

"The parade!" exclaimed Tyler.

His mom nodded. "But I guess Gus and I won't be marching this year!"

Tyler always felt proud watching his mom and her dog lead the other police officers down the street. In fact, he loved everything about the parade: floats, fire engines, and high-stepping horses. Sometimes he even wished that he and Max belonged to a club or could do tricks so that they could march too.

But rescuing Pippa was more important than a month of parades.

The road ended at the fairground parking lot. It was full, and nearly every vehicle in it was a van: vans for cotton candy and popcorn; changing-room vans for acrobats and clowns; vans full of toys and prizes; vans for selling arts and crafts, homemade brownies, and homegrown apples.

And one van hiding a stolen poodle.

Tyler's mom got Gus out of the car and gave his spare leash to Tyler for Max. "It's too hot for you to stay in the car," she said, "but remember, this is police business. You and Max are not to get involved!"

Tyler nodded.

Max didn't.

They started around the outside edge of the parking lot, Gus striding proudly in front, sniffing each vehicle as he passed. Tyler and Max had to jog to keep up.

The parade was about to start. Tyler paused to watch. Bands were playing, jugglers were juggling, clowns were clowning, and dogs in sparkly collars were quivering on their leashes. Crowds were streaming through the exit, racing for the best spots along the parade route.

Suddenly Max began to bark.

As the dachshund's deep voice echoed through the parking lot, a man sprinted toward the parade, knocking over a baby in a stroller and two kids on bikes. There was a flash of silver as he threw something into the ditch beside the parking lot exit . . . and then he disappeared into the crowd.

"Not good!" said Tyler's mom in a voice that meant she was so angry she was scared she'd say something really bad. "If we'd found the vehicle, I could have sent Gus after him, but I don't have anything for Gus to sniff!"

"I might," said Tyler. "I found this in Pippa's dog door." He pulled the scrap of navy blue material out of his pocket.

His mother took it and grinned. "Thanks, partner—that's exactly what we need! It'll have the dognapper's scent on it—Gus can easily track it."

She held the scrap out for the big dog to sniff. "Seek!" she commanded, and disappeared into the crowd with Gus.

"Stay here!" she called over her shoulder to Tyler. "If I'm not back in ten minutes, call Mrs. Lacey!"

But Max was already tugging Tyler forward. In the next row of vehicles was a gray van with dirty license plates and windows up against its roof. Every few seconds, the tips of two floppy, creamy ears floated into the window and down again.

As they reached the van, they could hear excited yipping.

"Pippa!" Tyler shouted. He grabbed the back door handle and pulled—but the van

was locked tight. Even the windows were sealed shut. The air inside would soon be dangerously hot. They had to get her out before that happened!

"Keys!" thought Tyler, remembering that flash of silver. He raced back to the exit with Max and jumped down into the ditch.

The keys weren't there—they had to be in the pipe under the road. Tyler threw himself onto his stomach to peer into it. He couldn't see anything except black; he couldn't reach anything except mud and slime.

He wiggled back, and Max wriggled in.

Ten minutes later, a slimy black nose appeared at the other end of the pipe. A long, muddy body slinked out. Clamped tight in a strong, muddy jaw was a key ring with one dangling silver key.

They raced back to the van. Pippa yipped once, but she'd stopped leaping.

The key worked. The door swung open.

Twelve black poodles rushed to greet them.

Tyler had been so sure he'd seen Pippa that he'd broken into a stranger's van. Where was the cream-colored poodle now?

But while Tyler was still figuring out what to do, Max had hopped into the van. Now he was bursting with joy: licking, sniffing, and dancing with one of the black poodles, exactly the way he did with Pippa.

The tips of this poodle's ears were pale and creamy.

"Pippa?" said Tyler, and the black poodle with creamy ears jumped to his shoulders, with her arms around his neck.

Tyler patted her, and his hand came away black.

"So that's why the dognapper went to the hairdresser's!" Tyler said. "But he didn't take Pippa in with him; he just bought the dye!"

The van was getting hotter and hotter. The dogs were panting, and there was no water. He had to get them out of there.

A long rope was coiled under the front seat. Tyler tied it to the handle of Max's leash and then looped a leash length through the ring on Pippa's collar and knotted it too. One by one, he took the poodles out of the van, tying the rope to each collar so that all twelve poodles were strung out in a long line behind Max. There was just enough rope left for him to hold.

He looked around the parking lot. His mom was nowhere in sight. It had been more than ten minutes since he'd seen her—time to call Mrs. Lacey.

Except that his phone was on Mrs. Lacey's kitchen table. And he couldn't even stay where he was, because thirteen thirsty dogs were pulling him to a water trough at the start of the parade.

The band was already blaring its way down the street, followed by two rows of police officers and firefighters, a row of kids twirling batons, and horses with white-shirted, red-cowboy-hatted riders.

Clowns and jugglers tumbled along, weaving in and out of the groups of marchers. One of the clowns ran right to the start of the parade, grabbing the bandleader's baton and conducting wildly.

The crowd laughed and cheered—and then gasped as an enormous German shepherd leapt into the air and knocked the clown to the ground. It held him there until Officer Olson ran up to clap handcuffs onto the clown's wrists. Two other police officers stepped out of the line to help her, and the crowd cheered again, thinking it was all part of the parade.

Tyler's mom looked up and saw Tyler being towed by Max and twelve poodles. The poodles ran even faster when they saw the handcuffed clown, passing everyone till they were nearly at the front, right behind the band.

So Tyler, Max, and the twelve black poodles followed the band and led the marching police officers and firefighters, the baton-twirling kids, and all the rest of the parade. It was a long route, right through the town, past houses and apartment buildings, past the town hall, hospital, and schools, past corner stores and shopping malls.

The band marched to the bandstand in the middle of the park to play one final song. Tyler looked around the crowd. He couldn't see his mother, he was hot and thirsty, and he had thirteen dogs at the end of a rope.

Suddenly he heard the wail of police sirens. Four police cars pulled up, and his mom and Gus ran to the bandstand.

Mrs. Lacey and eleven other people got out of the cars and followed them.

The poodles began to yip and dance on their rope, tugging Tyler toward the bandstand.

A policeman came over to help him. He winked at Tyler as Mrs. Lacey and the eleven other people climbed up onto the bandstand. Officer Olson started to speak.

"As you know, there has been a spate of dognappings in this town," she said. "We believe we have the dogs here, even though these poodles are black, and the stolen dogs were all different colors.

"Tyler," she continued, "could you please untie the first dog?"

Tyler untied the poodle closest to his end of the rope. In two bounds, the little black poodle flew up the steps to Cassandra Caniche, as if she were the only person on the bandstand.

One by one, Tyler let the other poodles off. One by one, they raced straight to someone on the bandstand, until Mrs. Lacey and the black poodle tied next to Max were the only ones left alone.

Tyler untied the last loop.

The little dog flew into Mrs. Lacey's arms, wrapping her front paws around her owner's neck and covering her face with licky kisses.

"I think you can see," Tyler's mom said finally, over the noise of licking and yipping, patting and sobbing, "that even if humans might not have been able to work it out, the dogs knew who they belonged with!"

Another policeman came up and handed her a message. Tyler's mom scanned it quickly.

"The dognapper has confessed. After last year's fair, when Cassandra Caniche won prizes for the Best-Groomed Poodle, the Best-Spun Poodle Wool, and the overall Best Item for a poodle wool coat, the dognapper asked her to marry him. When she said no, he threatened that she'd never again have the glory of winning so many prizes. So, two weeks ago, he teased Cassandra's dog with fresh, juicy steak until it followed him out into his van. He then stole all the other poodles in the same way. He dyed them black so no one would recognize them—and so he could win the Best-Matched Poodles prize tomorrow! Fortunately we arrested him first. When he heard what he thought was a police dog, he ran away, knocked down a clown, and stole his costume. But he'd left behind a scrap of his shirt when he stole the last poodle— and so the real police dog knew who he was."

"Hooray for Gus!" shouted someone who'd seen the police dog tackle the clown.

Gus lifted his head proudly, and Tyler's mom patted him. "Gus caught him," she agreed, "but the true hero is the dog who tracked him down and rescued the poodles."

Everyone was surprised, because everyone knew there was only one police dog in the town.

"Max!" called Tyler's mom.

The little dachshund had tracked a vehicle

and run for more than an hour, dug two tunnels and searched a drain, found his friend, and led a parade of lost poodles through the streets of the town. He was sound asleep.

But he woke up when Officer Olson called, and he followed Tyler up the steps on his strong stumpy legs.

The policeman who'd brought the message stepped forward and held up a small gold tag.

"In recognition of Max the Dax's outstanding service today, I'm awarding him the title of honorary police dog."

He threaded the tag onto Max's collar.

The crowd cheered; Cassandra Caniche and all the other people who'd been reunited

with their poodles hugged Tyler while their dogs licked Max. Mrs. Lacey kissed them both. Tyler's mom and the other police officer shook Tyler's hand and Max's paw.

Gus leaned down and licked Max's head. And Max licked him back.

Because of Shoe

by Pam Muñoz Ryan

illustrated by Olga and Aleksey Ivanov

Shoe

I cannot talk. And that's not like me.

I am at the beach with my family: my
mom and Theo; our little poodle, Lucky; and
my German shepherd, Shoe, who is leaping
over small waves like a jackrabbit. Shoe is
soaked to the bone. Suddenly she stops and
turns to look back at me, tilting her head to
the side. I know what she's thinking. She's

thinking it's strange that I'm not talking, because usually I never stop. But after what happened today, my heart is puffed up with emotion, like a balloon about to burst, and I'm afraid if I say anything, I'll start to cry. See, earlier, at the courthouse, everything changed. And it was all because of Shoe.

"Can you tell the court your name?" asked the judge. His black robe, long face, and dark bushy eyebrows made him look like a vulture.

"Lilianna Parker," I said from the witness stand. "But everyone calls me Lily."

The courtroom was filled with adults and other children who had come to court with their own petitions and waited to sit before the judge.

"And, Lily, how old are you?"

"Eleven years old."

The judge put on his glasses and peered at me.

"I know," I said. "I look younger. I'm the shortest in my class. That's my mom over

there." I pointed across the room to where Mom sat at a wooden table. "She's a nurse at Memorial Hospital, and she's barely over five feet. My pediatrician says that when I grow up, I will only be a tiny bit taller. But I'm *really* hoping he's wrong. Anyway, my freckles and thin hair don't help either. Plus, I'm trying to grow out my bangs because I think that *no* bangs will make me look more like a fifth-grader, which I *am*, instead of a third-grader, which I am *not*."

The judge smiled. His cheeks puffed up like peaches, his eyes twinkled, and he didn't look like a vulture anymore. He looked like someone's grandpa. "Well, Lily, let's move on. We're not going to be too formal here today. Can you tell us about the circumstances that brought you to my courtroom?"

I looked at Mom. She nodded encouragement. Mom had already coached me, but not about lying, since I wouldn't do that anyway. Instead she had given me the talk about keeping my answers brief, which is really hard for me. I always tell way too much information. Mom said, "Make the long story short." And I promised I would try, I really *would*. But my mind had a mind of its own.

"Lily?" said the judge.

I nodded, twisting a long strand of brown hair around one finger and trying to find a beginning. "It all started about a year ago, with Shoe."

The judge looked puzzled. "A shoe?"

I sat a little straighter. "No, not *a* shoe. Our *dog*, Shoe. We adopted her from the Coastal Humane Society. See, I had been wanting a dog for a long time, and finally Mom thought it would be a good idea. She said we should get one for protection since we were two girls living alone, on account of my father disappearing off the face of the planet before I was born. Besides that, I was spending more time at home by myself because I didn't go to after-school care anymore. But believe me, I wasn't a latchkey kid because our next door neighbor, Mrs. Gonzalez, was always checking on me. But Mom said that she'd feel more comfortable if there was a dog in the house. We really couldn't afford a dog from the pet shop, and even if we could pay eight hundred dollars, Mom wouldn't do it. She thinks everyone should adopt from animal shelters because of the current dog population, which is extremely high. She also has this thing about overbreeding."

I glanced at Mom. She was gently tapping the side of her cheek with one finger.

That was a signal that meant Too Much Information.

I took a deep breath, which is what I was supposed to do if she signaled me. "So we went to the Humane Society, and the minute I saw Shoe, I knew that she was the dog for me. I put my face near hers, and I just asked her, 'Do you belong to me?' And I know you're not going to believe this, but she answered. I mean, not in English, but you know, in the way she *looked* at me. Mom said that from day one, Shoe and I had this secret communication thing. So we adopted her. At first, we could not decide what to name her, but then—"

The judge held up his hand. "Lily, I need to interrupt for a moment. Does the dog's name have *anything* to do with why we're here today?"

I nodded vigorously. "Oh, yes. It has *every-thing* to do with it!"

Some of the people in the courtroom chuckled.

Mom rolled her eyes.

"Then you may continue," said the judge, leaning back in his chair.

"Okay. So we adopted her, and as soon as we brought her home, she started this thing with shoes. She would sneak into a closet, and I mean that entire skulking thing that dogs do when they don't want to be noticed. She would pick up a shoe in her mouth and then run out of the room. Then we'd have to chase her to get it back. But a few hours later, she would do the same thing. It's not that she chewed on the shoes or wrecked them or anything. And when I asked her, 'Why are you doing that?' she pulled the shoes closer to her chest, crossed her paws over them, and laid her head down and licked them. See, she thought they were *puppies*."

The judge leaned forward. "Puppies?"

A smattering of giggles traveled through the courtroom.

"Yes! It was the weirdest thing. She carried the shoes to her favorite places, like, behind the couch or the back of a closet. Then when she had a pile of them, she'd protect them and nose them and even *talk* to them. Not human talk, of course, but dog talk. You know, whining and little barks. So, Mom and I had to put all of our shoes up on the closet shelves. But then Shoe sniffed the floor, and whined, and looked at me and Mom with the saddest eyes and said, 'I'm begging you, please give me some shoes.' We couldn't resist. I gave her my soccer shoes that were too small, and Mom gave her a pair of high heels she never wore because she said they hurt her feet and when did she go dancing anymore anyway?"

Mom cleared her throat.

That was another signal. If I heard Mom clear her throat, I was supposed to pause and think about what I *needed* to say, not what I *wanted* to say.

"So Mom and I started calling her Shoe

Mama, because of her shoe puppies. But eventually we just called her Shoe. After a few months, she grew out of the whole pretending-shoes-were-puppies thing. It was like she just woke up one day and said, 'Oh, silly me. These are *shoes*, not my babies.' And just like that, she wasn't interested in shoes anymore. Until the incident."

"The incident?" asked the judge. His forehead wrinkled with concern.

I nodded. "But that came later. See, when we adopted her, the people at the Humane Society said they didn't know exactly how old Shoe was. They *thought* she was about a year old and wouldn't grow much larger. But they were so wrong. She grew a lot more. The vet said she was one of the biggest German shepherds he'd ever seen *in his whole entire life.* Everyone said she was too much dog for us. But we couldn't take her back because by then, she already loved us and we loved her. And besides, how could I give back a dog who reads my mind?"

"She reads your mind?" asked the judge.

I nodded. "Yes! I can just look at her and *think* that she needs a walk, and she will go sit next to her leash. Or one time I couldn't find my backpack and I was looking all over the house for it, but I wasn't saying, 'Where's my backpack?' I was just *thinking* it. And Shoe started whining and pawing at the door. When I opened it, my backpack was right there on the back steps. See what I mean?"

The judge nodded. "I think so. Let's get to the incident."

"Okay. So Shoe started being really protective of Mom and me. If anyone came near us, she went ballistic with her barking." I leaned closer to the judge and whispered, "For a while, Grandma wouldn't even come to our house because she was so scared of Shoe."

The judge raised his eyebrows and nodded knowingly.

Mom cleared her throat *and* tapped her cheek.

I took a deep breath and thought about what I *needed* to say. "Okay. So the Humane Society offered obedience training on Saturdays at Ocean Bay Park. We took Shoe to the first class, and there was this humongous line of people with their dogs, and it was hardly moving because once you got to the front of it, you had to fill out all these forms. The guy in front of us was thin and over six feet tall, which is *really* tall for short people like us. He had curly black hair and black glasses and was wearing workout clothes, but he wasn't sweaty or smelly or anything like that. He had on running shoes with those short socks, and a T-shirt from some marathon, the type you can only get if you actually *run* one. What was funny was that he was holding this weensy white poodle. This great big tall guy and this itty bitty dog. Mom and I were standing a little bit away from him because of personal space. And because people sometimes get nervous when Shoe is too close to them. But Shoe kept tugging on her leash, straining and whining and trying to move as close to him as possible. Finally, the man turned around and said to Mom, 'If you act like the pack leader, your dog will calm down.' Mom started laughing, and it *was* kind of funny. Because after all, we were in line for *obedience school.*"

The judge nodded. He took off his glasses, pulled out a handkerchief, and began cleaning the lenses. "What happened next?"

"Well, by this time Shoe was all hyper and jumping from one side of Mom to the other. So the guy does this amazing thing. He points at Shoe and says, 'Sit!' And Shoe *sat*! Mom and I were so surprised because Shoe *never* obeyed. Mom said, 'If you're so good at making a dog obey, why are you here?' "

The judge put his glasses back on. "Why *was* he there?"

"He said he was really good with big dogs. But that he'd never had a little dog in his life. See, the poodle would have never been his *choice* for a dog. He *inherited* it from a neighbor, a little lady who lived next door. The guy was always driving her—the lady, not the poodle—to the store and to the bank and fixing stuff around her house, and so when she died, she left her dog to him *in her will*. So how could he say no? But the poodle had some . . . uh . . . problems, like taking the guy's laundry outside—even his underwear— and leaving it in the street. And being afraid of feathers. If the poodle even *saw* one on the ground or especially floating in the sky, it started trembling and crying, and it was pitiful." I put my hand on my throat.

"Are you okay?" asked the judge.

"Yes. Sometimes when I talk too much, I start to gulp air and then I have to rest."

"Anytime you're ready," said the judge.

I massaged my throat and then began again. "So, we were at the park standing in line. The little poodle was wearing a tag with its name on it. Mom reached over to pat the poodle and said, 'Lucky? Your name is Lucky? I should have adopted a little dog like you.' And at that moment, the poodle leapt into Mom's arms, nuzzled into her neck, and started licking her ears. Mom was cooing and holding the poodle like a baby and tickling his tummy. And that's when it happened."

The judge leaned forward.

"While Mom was going all crazy for Lucky, Shoe stood up and walked a little closer to the man and sniffed around his feet. Then she looked up at me. I bent down and said, 'What is it, Shoe?' She looked at the man and looked at Mom and then at me, and it was like *she knew*."

The judge's forehead crinkled. "Knew what?"

"That we were all MTBT. Sometimes dogs just *know*. And Shoe wanted to do something about it. So she did."

"MTBT?"

"Meant to Be Together."

The judge nodded slowly. "Okay. And what did Shoe *do*, exactly?"

Everyone in the courtroom leaned forward.

I took a deep breath. "Shoe squatted and peed right on his shoes."

There was a collective gasp and then a burst of laughter.

"Oh, my," said the judge.

"I know! Mom was seriously horrified. Shoe had never done *anything* like that before. And Mom didn't know this guy or how he'd react. Or if he'd be furious or even *sue* us."

"What *did* he do?" asked the judge.

"He just stared at his shoes. The pee was streaming down the outsides *and* the insides and soaking into his socks and everything. Then he stared at mom *and laughed.* He just laughed. And then Mom began to laugh too, and she kept saying, between laughing, 'I'm so sorry.' And he kept saying, 'Really, it's okay.' And Mom said, 'No, no, it's not okay.' When they were finally taking deep breaths and calming down, he looked at me and asked, 'What's your dog's name?' When I said, 'Shoe,' he looked at Mom and they started all over again, but this time they were laughing so hard that they were all bent over and holding their stomachs. I mean, a dog named Shoe pees on his *shoes.*"

The judge smiled. "Yes, I see the irony."

"Somehow, I ended up holding the little poodle and Shoe's leash because Mom and the guy were hysterical. And all this time, Shoe was being absolutely well-behaved. She was just sitting there calmly at my side, smiling. Some people say dogs don't smile. But I promise you, Shoe was smiling."

A side door to the courtroom opened, and

a clerk walked up to the judge and handed him a paper. "Your honor, the schedule is quite full today."

"How long do we have left?"

"About ten minutes," said the man.

The judge turned to me, "Lily, can you wrap it up in ten?"

I swallowed and nodded. "So I just stood there, holding Shoe's leash and Lucky, and watching my mom and this guy laughing so hard they were crying. I was surprised at Shoe because it wasn't good dog manners to pee on someone's shoes. But the thing that was the *most* surprising was hearing my mom laugh like that."

"Why was that surprising, Lily?" asked the judge.

"Well, see, it's been really hard for her taking care of me by herself all these years. She hardly ever did anything like go out with people her own age or on a date. Not that guys didn't ask her out. They did. And sometimes she went out with them, but so far, they'd been *so* not her type. And Shoe didn't like *any* of them. There was this one guy who only talked Mondays, Wednesdays, and Fridays. And another who only ate orange food for dinner. Oh, and one who whistled through his nose when he breathed."

Mom was practically coughing from clearing her throat, and her cheek was pink from all the tapping.

I took two deep breaths and paused for a second. "She sort of gave up dating and just concentrated on me. And that was okay. I was her top priority. Sometimes, though, I wanted someone special, besides me, to concentrate on *her*. That day in the park, it was so nice. The way he was holding her arm and looking at her and laughing with her was nice . . . really nice."

"I can imagine it was," said the judge.

"You want to know a secret?" I asked.

The judge had his elbow on his desk and had his chin resting in his hand. "Yes, Lily, I actually do."

"Kids *really* like to hear their parents laugh because it means they have happiness in their hearts. See, most of the time parents' hearts are all filled up with responsibility and seriousness. When Mom was laughing out loud in the park, all I could do was just stand there and listen and smile, because . . . well . . . it was like a favorite song I hadn't heard in a really long time."

The courtroom was very quiet. I wasn't sure how many minutes I had left, but I started talking right away because there was more I *wanted* and *needed* to say. "See, it's kind of amazing how much you can learn about a complete stranger by simply standing in line with him and watching your dog pee on his shoes. We were really lucky that the line was so long, too, because by the time we got to the registration table, Mom discovered that the guy's name was Theodore Ochoa, but everyone called him Theo, and that he knew one of Mom's friends from the hospital. And what were the chances of that? He lived practically in our neighborhood and sometimes jogged by our house. He said he used to have a dog who ran with him, but that dog died, and he missed having a friend at his side. To make a long story short . . ." I looked up at the judge to see if he got my joke.

He winked at me.

"Theo started stopping by to take Shoe for a run. And Shoe just *loved* Theo, but not as much as she loved me, of course. And when he took Shoe for a run, Mom and I would dogsit Lucky. We just made sure to put away the feather duster. And sometimes Theo would stay for dinner. And well, one thing led to another."

There was a tiny smile on Mom's face.

"Lily, let me get this straight. Your mom married Theo—"

"Yes."

"And that's why you have petitioned the court?"

"Yes. Since Theo's last name is Ochoa, and now Mom's last name is Ochoa, I'd really like to be an Ochoa, too. But the rule is that you have to get permission to change your name from all the parents listed on your birth certificate, even if you've never met them in your entire life. And if you can't, you have to come to court so the judge—that's you—can decide if it's in my best interest. I hope you decide that it is, because all I ever had for a father was a name on a piece of paper. And that's not very real."

I looked at Mom and thought about how happy Theo had made her and me. "See, *real* is the father who does stuff with you, like drive you to soccer practice, and go for walks on the pier with you and your dog, and help you with your homework, and bring you a quilt when you're cold in the middle of the night. That's the one who is real."

The judge took off his glasses again—not to clean them but to blot his eyes. "And where is Theo now, Lily?"

"He's waiting right out in front of the courthouse with Shoe and Lucky so that if we need him, he can trade places with Mom at a moment's notice."

"That won't be necessary, Lily," said the judge. "You're the only one I need to talk to today."

"Afterward, no matter what your decision, we're going to Dog Beach, where you can let your dogs off leash to run around and play and jump in the waves. We can take Lucky now, even though there are a lot of bird feathers on the sand, because we did behavior therapy with him. And Shoe hasn't peed on *one other person.*"

"Well, I'm glad to hear it," said the judge.

The clerk came back into the courtroom.

The judge turned to me. "Lily, I think you've given me enough information to make my ruling. You made my job easier today. You may step down."

I slipped out of the witness stand and went to Mom's side. The judge made his decision and passed the paperwork to the clerk, who passed it to Mom, who smiled.

There was something happening inside me, something filling me up with so much emotion that my throat felt tight. I couldn't say good-bye to the judge. All I could do was hold up my hand and bend my fingers in a tiny wave. Mom stood up and put her arm around me, and we headed out of the courtroom.

The clerk called the name of another child, and he and his family took our places. I hoped they would have a good outcome.

Outside, Theo was waiting on a bench. Shoe sat next to him and he held Lucky in his arms. Lucky started wiggling as soon as he saw us.

Theo drove us to Dog Beach, and Mom held Lucky in her lap. I sat in the back seat with Shoe. Each time I looked at her, she tilted her head to the side and stared at me. I stroked her chest and talked to her with my eyes. When we arrived at the beach, Shoe and Lucky jumped from the car and ran toward the water. I held back and walked hand-in-hand with Theo and Mom.

"You're awfully quiet, Lily," said Theo. "That's not like you. Everything okay? Do we need to see a doctor? Do you have a temperature? You know, your mom has connections at the hospital."

I smiled.

Shoe races toward me, wet from the waves. She stops at my side and shakes. Droplets spray over me. I bend over and put my face near hers. Wildly, her tail wags, and she licks my cheek. I want her to be the first to hear. I whisper, "Lily Ochoa."

Shoe leaps back and plants her front legs apart, then jumps forward again, egging me on. Suddenly, I don't feel like being quiet anymore. I spread out my arms. Shoe runs, and I chase her. This time, I yell into the ocean breeze. "Lily Ochoa!"

Lucky barks. Shoe barks louder.

Mom and Theo laugh.

All my happiness spills over, and as usual, my mind has a mind of its own. I yell my new name again, and again, and again.

Science Fair

Written and illustrated
by Mark Teague

Howard

Soon after Judy Nussenbaum moved in next door, Howard Eubanks became a dog. To most people in Fenwick Grove, the events were unrelated. Boys rarely became dogs, after all, and Howard's transformation was considered a sad and mystifying event. But Judy didn't think so, and neither did Howard. Every time she walked by his house, he barked.

"It's not my fault!" she called from her own front yard. "How was I supposed to know it would work?"

The question was unanswerable, especially by Howard. But even in his dim, doggy state, he blamed her.

The day they met, Howard was working in his lab, as usual. When Judy pounded on the front door, he emerged from the basement, blinking like a mole. "What do you want?"

"Mom says we have to go outside." She had frizzled hair and pointy elbows. Sunlight glinted on her braces.

"I don't even know you."

"I'm Judy Nussenbaum. Who're you?"

"Howard Eubanks, and I'm busy. The science fair is in two days. Now go away."

For Howard, the science fair at Arturo V. Mortensen Middle School was the year's most important event. Twice he'd entered and twice—inexplicably—he'd lost.

His first attempt came in sixth grade. He was sure he'd win. All year he'd been winning chess tournaments and debate tournaments and spelling bees. He'd programmed his clock radio to send signals in Morse code. He translated the Gettysburg Address into Egyptian hieroglyphs. Everyone knew he was a genius. The *Fenwick Times* featured him in an article titled "Ten Kids to Watch Out For."

"I'm simply better than everyone else," he confided to his diary.

And yet, somehow, Monique Moldinado won first prize at that year's fair. Her invention, a tap-dancing robot, took the event by storm. After renditions of "I've Got Rhythm" and "Mr. Bojangles," it brought down the house with a spirited performance of "Singin' in the Rain."

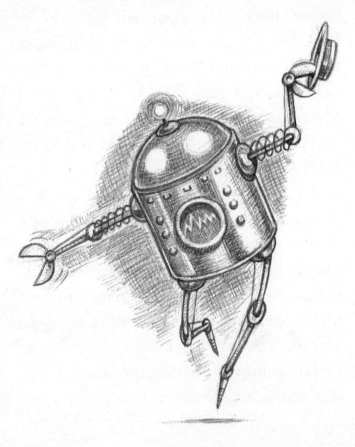

Howard had to settle for honorable mention. His solar-powered pooper-scooper was a remarkable and useful device, but it couldn't dance.

"Don't listen to them," said Mr. Von Epps, his science teacher, when Howard's classmates giggled. "Foolish people may call you names, but you must never be deterred."

"De-TURD!" gasped Wayne Funderberg, as if he'd been handed a precious gift.

"De-TURD! De-TURD!" chanted the rest of the class.

The nickname stuck. "My school is infested with morons," wrote Howard.

The worst thing about morons was that they were too dumb to know they were morons. They were even too dumb to know that he, Howard, was made of finer stuff. "I will have to show them," he wrote.

He began planning for next year's fair. As a demonstration of behavioral science, he trained a dozen chicks to play "Jingle Bells" on a piano. "Let's see Monique Moldinado top that!" he wrote. But it was Tommy Alvarez who won first prize. Flown by a crew of hamsters, his miniature zeppelin was a triumph. The crowd went wild. The hamsters danced in their tiny cockpit.

Meanwhile, Howard learned that chicks, however musical, cannot be house-trained. The mess they made on the keyboard brought a familiar chant.

"De-TURD! De-TURD!"

"Cretins!" Howard wrote. "They ridicule what they don't understand."

What he could not understand was how Monique Moldinado and Tommy Alvarez could have beaten him. He was the genius, after all. And geniuses never quit!

"My final attempt," he wrote, "will be the greatest achievement in the history of science fairs!"

So Howard brooded while the chicks grew to rangy adulthood. At night he lay awake, scheming, while roosters crowed in his backyard. He realized that training birds had been a mistake. Nobody liked poultry. If he wanted to win, he would need rodents, like Tommy Alvarez.

A plan took shape in his mind. He Googled information on genetics. He learned everything he could about DNA and RNA, chromosomes and mitochondrial extraction. He bribed the Trevinos' bulldog, Larry, with ham bones so that he could scrape skin cells from its tongue. He constructed a laboratory in his basement and disappeared for days on end. He manipulated chromosomes and spliced genes. He injected his mouse with formulas derived from mutant dog cells. He cackled. His brilliance would shock the world!

The fair approached. Howard was just one step away from dazzling his fellow students with the world's first dog-mouse. He worked harder. Dark circles appeared under his eyes.

Then Judy Nussenbaum showed up.

"Go away!" he repeated. "I'm at a critical point in my experiment."

"Snotty." She peered through the screen door. "You got a lab down there?"

"Yes, and it's quite extensive. As I said, the science fair is in two days."

"I'll probably win that," she said in an off-hand way.

Howard's face reddened. "You will not! The fair is highly competitive."

"So am I. If you're lucky, maybe I will help you."

"Like I need your help!"

She examined him closely. "Trust me, you do."

"You're the one who needs help," said Howard. "As in psychiatric help. For your information, I'm doing research that will change the whole world."

"Uh-huh." Judy yawned. "What did you do for last year's fair?"

The question surprised him. "I taught chicks to play 'Jingle Bells' on a piano."

"Well, that's sort of interesting. Where'd you get the little pianos?"

"Stupid! There weren't any little pianos! It was a dozen chicks on a regular-sized piano. Each one pecked a separate note."

"Chickens are dumb," she said. "Your roosters keep me awake all night."

"Never mind chickens. This year I'm doing something much more sophisticated. I'm going to create a dog-mouse."

"A dog-mouse, huh? Will it dance?"

"No, it won't dance!" Howard slammed the door.

Back in his lab, he was unable to concentrate. Had he said too much? What if Judy Nussenbaum really did have a plan to win the fair? Could she be another Monique Moldinado or Tommy Alvarez? "Don't let it happen again!" he wrote in his diary. That night he slept fitfully. The roosters crowed.

Judy caught up with him the next morning on the way to school. Howard put his head down and sped up. The fair was coming. He mustn't be distracted.

"Look at the way you walk," she said. "All

hunched over. You might as well tape a 'kick me' sign to your back."

"Leave me alone."

"I wish I could," she said. "But I'm interested in you, and when I take an interest in something, I'm very persistent. Know what I'm going to do?"

"No. Nor do I care."

"I'm going to fix you so you aren't such a dwid. It's my new project."

"I'm not a *dwid*, whatever that is. For your information I was voted one of the *Fenwick Times'* Ten Kids to Watch Out For."

"Ten Dwids to Watch Out For," said Judy.

Across the street, Wayne Funderberg yelled, "De-TURD!"

"If you carry yourself with confidence, people won't think you're such a doofus."

"Why should I care what these halfwits think?" A corn muffin hit him in the chest.

"You care," said Judy. "Why else would you make a zombie mouse in your basement?"

"I'm not making a zombie mouse! And don't talk so loud. My project is a secret."

Someone yelled, "De-TURD has a girl-friend!" Someone else threw a banana. Judy caught it.

"See?" said Howard. "They don't like you, either."

"Not yet," Judy said calmly, eating the banana. "But they'll come around. People admire my originality."

Howard was sure that wasn't true. Still, it stuck in his mind. In English class he wrote a short story in which superintelligent aliens from another galaxy conquer Earth and enslave its people. They regard Earthlings as a grossly inferior race and treat them with contempt. The only exception is a single, brilliant boy named Broward. Unappreciated by his own race, Broward is greatly admired by the aliens, especially their princess, the lovely Xandra.

It was a terrific story until the princess started speaking. For some reason, she sounded exactly like Judy Nussenbaum. Howard erased her dialogue but could not figure out how to rewrite it. The story limped to an unsatisfying conclusion.

When the final bell rang, the kids ran out in a screaming mob. Howard followed cautiously.

Judy caught up with him by the flagpole. "Buy me an ice cream."

"Buy yourself an ice cream!" He hurried past her.

"I've been thinking about your experiment," she said. "A zombie mouse isn't much of a crowd-pleaser. You ought to consider doing something with more pizzazz."

"Oh, really! Like what?"

"I don't know. Why not drink the dog juice yourself? You could be like Lon Chaney."

"Who?"

"Lon Chaney. He played Larry Talbot in the original *Wolf Man*. He became a werewolf after Bela Lugosi bit him. It might be interesting if you could pull off something like that."

"Don't be ridiculous," said Howard. "That's not science, that's just a stupid movie."

"It's a scary stupid movie."

"It wouldn't make sense to drink the formula, either. The material must be injected."

"So inject yourself. You can be a dog for a few hours. It'd be an improvement, if you ask me."

"I didn't ask you. And for your information, genetic changes are permanent!"

"Only if you do it wrong."

"No, not if you do it wrong! You're so dumb! The only way to reverse the process would be to develop an antidote to restore the original genetic balance. Which has never been done, by the way."

"Chicken."

"I'm not a chicken. It's just that it would be crazy to experiment with something so dangerous."

"Cluck, cluck. Now I know why you have chickens in your backyard. They're part of your flock."

"You're insane," said Howard.

"Maybe. But at least I know how to win a science fair."

"You're not going to win!" Howard ran inside his house and slammed the door.

In the basement, he tried to calm himself. It wasn't easy. Even Wayne Funderberg wasn't as annoying as Judy Nussenbaum. He fiddled with his microscope for a while, then quit in exasperation. His dog-mouse looked up at him and wagged its tail.

"Boring!" muttered Howard. Somewhere in his mind a robot tap-danced. Hamsters steered a small zeppelin around a gymnasium. What was a dog-mouse compared to that?

But a dog-*boy*? That was interesting. That was something to make the kids at Mortensen sit up and take notice. He pictured himself strolling into school half dog, half boy, with shiny fur and glistening canines. Wayne Funderberg would scream. Monique Moldinado and Tommy Alvarez would turn green with envy. And Judy Nussenbaum—well, at least maybe she'd shut up for a while.

Almost without thinking, he began to calculate the formula. He spliced genes culled from Larry the bulldog and added the mixture to a mitochondrial solution and a sample of his own tonsils that he'd been saving since their removal three years earlier. He mixed the formula in a sterilized beaker. Would it work? Why not?

No! screamed some other part of his mind. *Are you mad?* The idea was too risky. And for what? To win a school science fair? He leaned on his workbench. What was he thinking?

It was Judy Nussenbaum. She was making him crazy. Before she showed up, he had been perfectly happy with his dog-mouse. More than just happy—he'd been euphoric! Whether the subhumans at Arturo V. Mortensen Middle School understood it or not, his project marked a turning point in science. He had invented a whole new species! The world would never be the same! And now here he was, nearly throwing it all away for the sake of mere showmanship!

He was about to dump his formula into the sink when his mother appeared in the doorway upstairs. "Howard, it's the girl next door! She wants to see you."

"Tell her I'm busy."

"I will not! Now, be a gentleman."

Moments later, Judy clomped down the stairs. The door closed behind her. "Hey, Frankenstein," she said. "What's cooking?"

"What do you think?" he muttered. "I'm working on my project."

She peered into the mouse cage. "It looks a little bit like a Chihuahua. I guess that's sort of interesting."

"More than I can say for you. If you even have your own project, that is."

"Mine's already done. I've got a volcano, lava, the whole shebang. Lots of razzle-dazzle. You need help with that dog juice? We could mix it with lemonade so it tastes better."

"I told you, I'm not changing myself into a dog!"

"Well, what's your dog-mouse going to

do? Fetch? Roll over? You need something that'll get the judges' attention."

"It's a genetically distinct species. That should be enough for any judge!"

"Yeah, right. Hey, let's go to the convenience store and buy some candy."

"No! I told you I'm busy!"

"Doing what? If you aren't going to win the fair, what's the point schlubbing around in this basement all day?"

Howard had an idea. "If I drink the juice, will you leave me alone?" He held up the beaker.

"What do you mean, 'alone'?"

"I mean will you go away and stop bugging me?"

"You'll drink that goop?"

"Every drop." Howard smiled to himself. Drinking the juice might not taste good, but it couldn't harm him. His body would simply digest it. It was injecting the material that could cause a problem. But dingbat Judy didn't know that.

"Deal," she said.

"Deal," said Howard, and he drank the beaker dry.

Judy watched him for a few minutes. Nothing happened. After a while Howard reminded her of their deal.

"All right, I'll go. That juice doesn't work anyway." She trudged back up the stairs. "See you at the fair."

Howard felt only a moment's relief. Then panic set in. Judy was right. His dog-mouse needed to do something! He tried training it: sit, fetch, roll over. Hours passed. He missed dinner. He went through handfuls of tiny dog treats. Without thinking, he ate some of the treats himself. The dog-mouse merely stared at him, tail wagging. "Hopeless!" he complained.

It was long past bedtime when his mother called for him to quit. "You can finish in the morning, dear."

Howard was too weary to argue. He staggered to his bedroom and turned off the light.

That night he had the oddest dreams. He chased squirrels and rode in a car with his head hanging out the window. Then he chased the car. Then the car chased him. Then he chased a bunch of squirrels inside a car. The car smelled funny. The squirrels smelled delicious! His hind leg jerked.

When he woke up, his body was covered in thin fur. A pink tongue lolled from the side of his mouth. His nose was cool and wet. "The fair!" he thought excitedly. "The fair! The fair!" Though his hands felt clumsy, he managed to get dressed and rush downstairs.

"Mouse!" he thought. "Mousemouse-mousemouse! Eat mouse!

"NO!" he corrected himself sternly. "Not eat mouse. Mouse for fair!" He grabbed the cage and bolted out the door.

"Name?" said the woman at the desk.

"Howard!" he woofed.

She wrote down "Woof" and directed him to a table where he could set up his presentation. It went badly. Trying to write a description of his project on index cards, Howard mangled the words. His paws had grown clumsy. He whined and licked his nose. He ate the pencil. "Mousemousemouse," he thought.

The other kids came in and set up their projects. Everyone was busy. Nobody noticed him. If they had, they would have witnessed a remarkable transformation. Howard's hands and feet shortened into stout paws, his ears flopped, his forehead flattened, and his coat grew thick and shiny. By the time the fair started, Howard was no longer Howard at all, but a bulldog wearing Howard's clothes. The clothes fit poorly. Even as a dog, he lacked pizzazz.

Judy was the only one who recognized him. "Howie?" she asked.

"Rowf?"

"Oh, Howie, it worked! Who knew? It really worked!" She ran to tell the judges, but they were unimpressed. Rules, they said, prohibited dogs from entering the science fair.

"But it's Howard Eubanks!" she said.

"Rules are rules," said Ms. Feldspar, the principal.

With Howard disqualified, Judy easily won first prize. Her experiment wasn't much, really, just a papier-mâché volcano that spewed steam from dry ice and melted cheese. But the sight of a village on the volcano's slope being engulfed by oozing Velveeta

Volcano
by
Judy
Nussenbaum

delighted the judges and thrilled the crowd. "JU-DY! JU-DY!" they chanted.

Howard was inconsolable. That afternoon he lay in the backyard with his feet in the air. He refused his kibble. He ignored the chickens. He growled at the crowd of reporters who appeared, seemingly from nowhere.

For two days the "dog-boy" story dominated the local news. "Could your child be next?" asked anchorwoman Mindy Sneffins.

Fortunately, the answer appeared to be no. When a family of Stone Age cave dwellers was discovered living in the hills west of Mungo, the reporters departed.

Things returned to normal, except that Howard was still a dog. And he was angry. He was angry with the school and the judges and the mailman (for no clear reason). But mostly he was angry with Judy.

"What did I do?" she asked.

"Growf!"

"It was your idea. I just encouraged you."

"Rowrowrow!"

"Well, anyway, you can't stay mad forever!"

Howard thought he could.

But Judy was persistent. "I passed around a petition," she said one day from behind the fence that separated their houses. "It says we think you should have won the science fair."

"Roop?"

"Sure. I got all the kids to sign. It was a great experiment, even if you didn't think it through very clearly."

"Broo!" Howard barked.

"Okay. Maybe I'm partly to blame. The point is, we all liked it." She slid a ham bone under the fence.

After she left, Howard chewed the bone thoughtfully. His tail began to wag.

Slowly he adjusted to life as a dog. It wasn't bad, really. He ate and slept and chased the chickens. Everything smelled wonderful. He developed a passion for squeaky toys.

After school (Howard had been expelled), Judy took him for walks. At the convenience store she bought candy and chewy bones. She told him about the day's events and about books she'd read and movies she'd seen. He tried to tell her about being a dog—the smells, the sounds, the pleasure of rolling in dirt—but it was difficult to explain. "Row-rowrowrop!"

They walked home with the leash loose between them. "I'm proud of you, Howie," she said. "It's hard to change. Lots of people just stay the way they are forever. Especially the dopey ones."

"Rodope!"

"Of course you were a dope. The only thing is, you may have changed too much."

"Arp!"

"I know, I know. You drank the dog juice. But, Howie, that juice should have been injected."

"Ri-no!"

"Everyone knows that's the way to make a genetic change. What you did shouldn't have worked at all."

"Arf!" he barked.

"Why did it work? I don't know. Maybe it's psychosomatic."

"Woof?"

"Psychosomatic. It means it's all in your head."

Howard knew what it meant—he just didn't believe it. "Fruff."

"Say what you want," said Judy. "It's the only thing that makes sense. You knew you were going to lose the science fair, so you were upset. And deep down, you were tired of being a dwid. Becoming a dog offered the only solution to the fix you were in. It was brilliant, really."

"Broof?"

"Broof. I mean it. But now you can stop."

Howard shook his head. Spittle flew from his jowls.

"You can, Howie. Trust me."

"Owruf."

"Of course you can. You can do anything you put your mind to."

So he did. Becoming human wasn't easy, the way it was for Lon Chaney in *The Wolf Man*. He had to improve his attitude. He had to stop thinking he was better than everyone else. He had to shed a *lot*.

His ears shrank, his fingers stretched, his fangs receded. He stared at the mirror.

Judy stared too. "I wish they could have seen this at the science fair."

But Howard no longer cared about science fairs. Not at all. He cared about clothes! He ran to his bedroom and threw on a pair of jeans and a shirt.

The next morning Judy walked with him to school. As they drew near, Howard began to fidget. He sniffed the air for flying muffins, but couldn't smell a thing. He tried twitching his ears, listening for the chant of "De-TURD! De-TURD!" but his ears wouldn't twitch, and the chant never came.

Instead, someone shouted, "Hey, everybody! It's Howie!"

A cheer went up. For a few glorious moments, it seemed as if the whole school had come out to welcome him back. Then a food fight started. Howard and Judy hurried to class.

For Howard, things did not get better all at once, but they did get better. Monique Moldinado smiled at him in the hallway. Tommy Alvarez offered him a ride in the new zeppelin he was building. Wayne Funderberg was hit in the head with a corn muffin, and nobody ever discovered who threw it.

And one day, as they were working together in the lab, Judy declared her project a success.

"What project?" asked Howard.

"Remember? I said I'd fix you. Well, I did it. You're not a dwid anymore."

"I'm not?" He watched his dog-mouse carefully. "Singin' in the Rain" played in the background.

"Not much, anyway. I'd say you're more of an original now, like me."

Howard smiled. It was good to be an original. If he'd had a tail, he would have wagged it. In its cage, his dog-mouse began to tap-dance.

Patty

Written and illustrated
by Thacher Hurd

Patty

Me and dogs.

Let's keep it simple.

Let's just say that I used to think one way about dogs, but after that trip to Grams and Grampa's last summer, things were a little different with me and dogs. Especially Patty. Just a little different.

I mean, I still think dogs slobber too much,

and we really need to do something about dog breath. Maybe it's time for some doggie mouthwash.

People seem to think dogs are the answer to all of life's problems. If we go running with our dog through sunlit fields of wheat like we're in a dog food commercial, then all our problems will be solved? I guess I'm supposed to like dogs. I'm a kid, and kids like dogs, right? We have a nice black Lab named Patty who wags her tail and gets all slobbery when I come home. My parents really like Patty a lot. They think she can do no wrong. I just wish she wouldn't want to slobber all over me when I give her a hug.

I don't want to make too big a deal out of this, but I have to mention that Patty may be sweet, but she also tends to throw up at strange times. Like the time my parents went out for a while but then they got delayed and it got dark.

I don't like being home alone at night. At first it's okay, but then I get the feeling the bogeyman is looking in the window.

So my parents go out, and all I do is go in my room and shut the door, and I make Patty come with me, and I won't let her out. She doesn't like that, but I feel nervous, and I end up in my bed with the covers pulled up high and my palms sweating, and I am thinking that every little noise in the house is someone coming up the stairs to chop me in little pieces and make me into soup.

Patty is supposed to be the watchdog, but then she starts getting nervous too, and she's pacing around my bedroom making little noises and then scratching at the door like she needs to go pee, but I know she doesn't because I just took her out right before I made her stay in my room. So I know she's faking that, and I don't want to let her out anyway, though if you think about it, it would probably be better if she was out roaming around the house being really fierce and all and protecting me with her big growl (which she doesn't really have) and her sharp teeth and her bad breath. I mean, her bad breath would drive anybody away.

But no, I keep Patty in my room, and I get more and more nervous, and my palms get sweatier and sweatier and then I hear a terrible noise, and I look out from under the covers.

Patty has thrown up. A big pile of throw-up in the middle of my rug. Great. It smells really bad, and I don't know what to do. Just then my parents come home and open the door to my room and smell the barf and then things get complicated. They say, "David, you shouldn't have done this," and "David, you shouldn't have done that," though all I did was get scared—the dog did the throwing up. But as usual, it's me in trouble, my parents petting the dog and looking down at me, and the dog looking up at me with those I-didn't-do-anything-I'm-just-the-dog eyes.

Maybe you're thinking at this point, Who are this kid's parents that they would leave him alone at night?

But the Lyonses live next door, and they're pretty helpful, except that Mrs. Lyons drinks twenty cups of coffee a day and vacuums her house twice a day and their son Robert is always cheating me out of stuff. One night at two A.M., when my parents *were* at home, I got up in my pajamas and bare feet and sleepwalked over to Robert's house and knocked on the door, and when his mother who drinks the twenty cups of coffee a day answered the door, I said, "Can Robert come out and play?"

Robert's mother walked me home in her nightgown and woke up my parents, and they put me to bed, and maybe they thought about putting a lock on the front door so I wouldn't escape. Patty slept through the whole thing. Patty doesn't sleepwalk. Just in her dreams. You can see her paws twitching when she's dreaming. Maybe she's running through sunlit fields of wheat.

Most of the time, my parents get a baby-sitter when they go out to dinner. I like it when Julie Saylor is the babysitter. She's funny and has blond hair, and she's only a few years older than me, and she likes to play games like poker. It was especially fun when she told me that joke about the two babies named Sam and Joe, twins in the womb. I was wondering how babies get in the womb in the first place, and it all seemed especially interesting because Julie looked so nice with her hair and her smile. Then she got to the punch line, where Sam and Joe come out of the womb (how does that happen?) and they look at each other and say, "Weren't we womb-mates?"

Julie and I laughed at the joke, and I thought it would be very exciting to be in the womb and have a twin brother named Joe because I don't have a brother. Or a sister, for that matter. All I have is Patty.

Then there are the other babysitters, like Mrs. Menzer. She's okay, but really old, like maybe fifty or something, and I like her, and she plays games with me, but she always gives me my dinner with the food mushed together on the plate so the mashed potatoes get mixed up with the vegetables, and the chicken gets mixed in too.

The worst babysitter was the old lady my parents found somewhere who looked like a witch. She only came once, and she wasn't very friendly. I didn't know who she was, and she came in a scratchy wool dress and had a pinched face. Everything was okay until I went to bed and turned out the light. Then somehow I got the idea that she *was* a witch or a really bad person and maybe she had a gun and she was going to come in my room and do something terrible. I lay in bed sweating just like I did when my parents left me alone with Patty, my mind going round and round, and I couldn't go to sleep. Then my parents came home, and everything was fine. They never knew that there had been the possibility that the babysitter was an evil witch. I feel like Patty should have at least barked once at the witch babysitter.

Last summer we drove way up north to visit my grandparents in their little house in the woods. That's where the big adventure happened, which was also all about Patty and me and being alone in the dark, except that this time Patty didn't throw up, not at all.

On the way up, I sat in the back of the car, and I made my own little cave out of a blanket. At first I wouldn't let Patty in, but she kept sticking her wet nose into the fort, so finally I let her in, and everything was fine until she decided to fart a big smelly fart, and I coughed and gasped, and she looked at me with those I'm-just-a-dog-I-can't-help-it-aren't-I-cute eyes, while I rolled down the window as fast as I could. Then Patty sat on my side of the seat and stuck her head out the window for the rest of the trip. She really likes that.

Finally we got to my grandparents' house in the country, and there was Yap Yap, their dog. Her name is Lucy, but I call her Yap

Yap, because it seems like no matter what is going on, she's barking. No matter how many times I've been to Grams's house, still Yap Yap barks at me and goes crazy as if I'm an evil intruder. She always has a pink sweater on, even in the summer. She's tiny, but she looks like she really wants to chomp on my ankle. Not to mention that last year she chewed up my copy of *A Wrinkle in Time* for no reason at all.

Grampa, who has this big mustache and always wears army boots, said to me, "The secret is, son, don't look at the dog. If you don't look at her, she won't feel threatened. Then she won't bark." He gave me a long lecture about why a dog is a man's best friend, but it was hard to concentrate on what he was saying, because Yap Yap was getting so thrilled and barky at the thought of taking a chunk out of my ankle.

One day on our visit, we went for a walk in the woods with Grams and Grampa. Their house is surrounded by a forest, and the year before, I got to make a fort in a big oak tree there, but now we were just going for a walk in the woods. I was thinking to myself, What is the point of this? Just walking? Why can't

we run, or be like woodsmen from the days of yore and hide behind trees and hunt deer and have terrifying adventures?

And then I thought, not knowing what was to come, The best would be if we got lost and there was a huge snowstorm, and everybody was about to die from the cold and snow, even Grampa, who is supposed to be such a great woodsman. But just in time I would step forward with bravery in my eye. Using our tracking skills, Patty and I would blaze a trail through the snow to the safety of a cave. We would all huddle by a fire that I would make by rubbing two sticks together. Then in the morning, everyone would pat me on the back and thank me for saving their lives. In the meantime, I would have discovered that the cave goes deep into the mountain, and I would uncover a strange native burial site with lots of artifacts in it, and the Museum of Natural History would give me a job, and I would work there and go on expeditions to Africa and Mongolia and dig up stuff. And Patty would come along, I guess. As long as she didn't throw up. That was my big brave thought.

But no, we were just going for a walk, and it didn't look like much of an adventure, so Patty and I were dawdling behind. Actually it felt kind of good to have Patty sticking close to me, her soft black fur against my leg.

We were walking through a little clearing when suddenly Patty put her nose in the air and started sniffing and then she ran straight into the woods, barking her head off. We called, "Patty! Patty!" and after a long time she stopped barking and came back. It looked like she had a white beard, and she wasn't barking—she was whimpering instead—and Grampa said, "I don't believe it. She's got into a porcupine."

Patty had all these quills in her mouth, and she looked really unhappy.

Grampa said, "We'll have to take her to the vet."

We started back toward home, but when we came to the big field behind Grams and Grampa's house, Patty took off again. We could see her chasing something black and white through the meadow. The black and white something raised its tail and then Patty came back to us, and she smelled so bad it was way, way beyond a bad smell. It was so bad it made you want to throw up, like a whole new universe of bad smell from the stinky planet. All together, we said, "Skunk!"

Now, right here you're thinking to yourself, That could never happen. A skunk and a porcupine in one day? Not one chance in a million.

But I didn't make this story up. We just hit the jackpot, the super double sweepstakes of smelly and porcupine, as my grandfather called it. Grampa drove my parents and me to the vet's with all the windows down and everyone holding their hands over their noses. Patty smelled so bad that the vet had to take the quills out in her garage. It was hard to watch, because it looked like it hurt Patty a lot. Even so, I could see Patty was really a brave dog, and she took it like a man, or a dog, I guess you would say. Afterward the vet washed Patty with something that looked like tomato juice to get rid of the skunk smell, but she still smelled crazy bad. I gave her a big hug anyway on the way back from the vet's, and Patty gave me a look like, "I'm really sorry. It's just my instincts. I'm a dog." And then I kissed Patty on her poor nose and said, "It's all right. You may be a dog, but you're a brave dog."

When we got home, everything was in an uproar. I mean, how could things get worse than they already were? But now Grampa thought he had put Yap Yap down in the field when we first saw Patty chasing the skunk, and then in the confusion had left her behind. Everyone had been so absorbed in Patty that they hadn't noticed how quiet things were. No yapping. You would think Yap Yap would bark her head off after being left behind, but . . . nothing. Maybe she was knocked out by a whiff of the skunk smell.

While we were at the vet's, Grams had been yelling and yelling for Yap Yap in the back meadow and walking around the fields calling, but no answer. She was kind of hysterical, and now it was late afternoon and we were all tired from the big day, but there was no way Grams and Grampa were going to let Yap Yap stay out all night. After all, she might get her little sweater dirty. Oh, sorry, didn't mean to say that.

So, even though it was late afternoon, it was time to organize a search party. Grams and Grampa and Dad and Mom and me and Patty. This time Grampa said we had to put Patty on a leash, so she wouldn't get into any more trouble, and I was on leash duty, bringing up the rear as we walked across the meadow to where Grampa thought he might have last seen Yap Yap. Grampa brought a couple of flashlights, in case we had to search all night or something.

We walked all the way through the field and didn't find Yap Yap, so we went on into the woods. Everyone began talking about where they thought they had seen Yap Yap earlier and what she must have been thinking, and how the poor little dog must be cold and shivering somewhere all alone. In her pink sweater, I thought. And not barking. That's a relief.

The whole time they were talking to each other, though, no one was thinking about Patty—Patty, whose ancestors were great hunters in England or somewhere, dogs who had amazing noses and could sniff anything from a mile away and find anything lost. But nobody was thinking about that; they were just trying to use their brains to find a brown dog with a pink sweater instead of using their noses, the way Patty would.

Grampa set off up a hill, saying that's where she must have gone. "We took her up that hill once, and she sat on the bench at the top of the hill, and she liked the wind in her fur. It's just a little ways up the hill, and if she's not there, we'll split up and search for her in teams. Maybe she's back in the field after all."

Grampa always likes to be the leader, the commander-in-chief.

Away we went, Patty and me following behind. I was wondering if her mouth was still hurting from all those quills, since she was holding back. She kept sniffing something off to the left, and the others started to get ahead of me. Then all of a sudden, Patty pulled hard on the leash and ran off sharp left, dragging me along behind her. I tugged on the leash to make her stop, but she just kept on and wouldn't let up.

Was it another skunk?

The branches were slapping my face as we went on, and I tripped on a log and went flying into the dirt. But Patty kept pulling. I got up, brushed myself off, and spat the dirt out of my mouth, and Patty took off again, zigzagging back and forth, her nose to the ground. At first we were running downhill, then the ground flattened out and we were in a pine forest, which was good because the trees were farther apart and I could follow Patty without getting my face whapped every two seconds.

By now I was thinking, Good dog, Patty, you'll find Yap Yap. I know you will. What else would make Patty run so fast?

I called out, "You're a real hunter, a real hunter. Nobody can find Yap Yap but you."

This seemed to get her going even faster. We kept running like this for a long time through the woods, and then I noticed that Patty was nosing back and forth in the same place, over and over, and then around in circles, and then . . .

She stopped and sat down.

I looked at her.

She looked up at me.

We listened. It was quiet in the woods. Just a little swishing in the pine trees. I looked at her again.

She'd lost the scent.

Maybe she still smelled too much like a skunk to smell anything else.

I listened some more. I couldn't hear my grandpa or my mom or dad. Patty moved a little bit. I told her to sit still, and I listened hard for a sound. But there was only the swish of wind in the trees. Nothing else. I looked around. The daylight was fading fast. I could hear an airplane high above.

A little part of my mind, a fear part, was getting bigger. I turned around in a full circle, peering into the woods. Everything looked the same. Which direction had we come from? What was Patty going after? Whatever it was, Yap Yap or something else, she had definitely lost the scent. She was just sitting there panting. My heart was pounding.

I sat down in the leaves and tried to think. Actually, I tried not to think. Not to think the one thing that my mind was already thinking: We're lost. And it's getting dark.

The trees were starting to fade into each other, turning into black angular shapes. Quiet all around. I petted Patty.

"Where are we?" I said.

She looked up at me with those big Patty eyes and shifted on her feet and then stared off into the woods. Was she afraid? Was she going to throw up like she did in my room? I started talking to her.

"It's okay, we'll get home. Patty, can you find the way home? Can you smell the way home?" Patty didn't move. She just looked off into the woods. No matter how hard I tried to get her to move, she just sat there on her haunches.

"Where is Yap Yap?" I whispered in her ear. Patty was like a statue—only her nose twitched a little.

We were lost, and Patty the wonder dog was definitely not coming through with a big batch of heroics. The dark trees looked darker, and the wind died down completely, and now it was definitely turning to night. I remembered something they taught us at camp about getting lost: Stay where you are. Don't try to find your way home. You'll just get more lost. At least that was what Counselor

Jake had said. Or I thought that was what he'd said. I wished I'd listened to what he was saying.

I sat down and leaned against the scratchy bark of a pine tree. Patty curled up next to me.

There was nothing to do but wait. I tried not to think about being in the woods all night, but in the back of my mind, the thought was looming, like a dark cloud. My palms were sweaty, and I wished I was at home curled up in bed with a good book and my dad downstairs listening to the stereo and everything right with the world.

Patty and I sat there for a long time, and then I saw the moon coming up through the trees. As it rose, the woods brightened, and light shone through the branches, and soon it seemed as bright as day. I could see anything in this light.

Anything at all.

Good, bad, or—

I heard a branch crackle, then another. Not far away. Just behind the tree I was leaning on. I peered around and saw a dark shape under a tree. Patty was up now, too, growling. Then she started barking, loud.

CRASH! The thing ran toward us, then stopped a few feet away and stood stock-still in the moonlight. Patty stopped barking. We both stared.

Then I saw its antlers.

A deer! Just as I realized what it was, it wheeled and ran gracefully away through the pines. Patty wanted to chase after it, but I grabbed her leash and held on tight, and this time she didn't get away from me.

My heart was still pounding. I stood for a long time, listening, then went back and sat down against the pine tree. Patty lay down next to me, and I put my arm around her and petted her head and felt her cold wet nose. Why do dogs have wet noses? Maybe it makes them better at smelling.

I looked up at the moon through the trees. The high branches rustled in a tiny breeze. Maybe the deer was just as afraid as I was.

I felt Patty's warm body next to mine. I rubbed her back, and she wagged her tail in the moonlight, and I remembered when my parents first brought Patty home. For a few years after our dog Trio died, we didn't have a dog, but then one night my parents went to their friends' house for dinner, and I was sleeping on the porch—and yes, don't worry, we had a babysitter—and it was really nice to be out there in the cool air in my sleeping bag. I had fallen asleep to the sound of the cars going by and, far away, a train. I woke up a little later when I heard my parents come home. The moon was shining that night, too.

Very quietly, they opened the porch door and slipped a little black ball of fur into my sleeping bag with me, and that was Patty, and she was our dog, our own little black Lab, and she had a cold wet nose and soft black fur just like now, far away and lost in the north woods.

Somehow, sitting there against that pine tree, I felt like we were going to be okay, Patty and me. I wasn't in a sleeping bag at home, but the night was beautiful and calm, and slowly I calmed down, too. After a long time, I fell asleep, even though the moon was so bright. I don't know how long I slept, but I woke to a sound in the distance.

Patty was up already, staring into the dark. I got up and turned, and though I couldn't see anything, I could hear a sound that was unmistakable and—

Irritating.

And wonderful. More wonderful than irritating at that moment.

Now it was close, cutting through the quiet of the pine forest: Yap Yap, barking that screechy, whiny bark.

Then I saw flashlights and heard my father calling, "David! David!"

I jumped up and down and called back and ran toward them and jumped some more and held Patty close and laughed, and soon they were all there, Mom and Dad and Grams and Grampa, hugging and happy and crying and everybody wanting to know what happened. I felt kind of stupid as I told the story, but no one seemed to mind that at all. When I finished, they put an old army coat of Grampa's on me and then we walked home in the moonlight.

I don't need to tell you the rest, except that Yap Yap hadn't been lost at all. She had walked home on her own and fallen asleep in the basket of clothes in Grams' laundry room, and no one thought to look there.

Ha!

I was hungry when we got back to Grams and Grampa's house, and nothing tastes better than scrambled eggs and toast at eleven-thirty at night, cooked the way Grams cooks them.

Then my mother tucked me into bed and gave me a long hug and cried a little bit but didn't say much, and I knew they had been through a lot looking for me—probably more than I had been through, actually. I lay in bed afterward, thinking, slowly unwinding my mind and getting used to the thought that everything was fine. That took a while.

I slept later than I've ever slept, and Patty did, too, and then the next day we said good-bye to Grams and Grampa, and Yap Yap barked as usual, but I did manage to get one pat in on her head before she tried to nip my finger.

Then we were headed home, Patty with her head on my lap as we drove down the interstate, her cold nose snuffling now and then, and no more smell of skunk, but every so often a whiff of her bad breath.

I wondered what it would be like if Patty and I could talk like friends talk. Just Patty and me. She definitely wouldn't talk in front of anybody else. That way we could share each other's secrets. We could lie on the hill behind the house and talk about what's really on our minds.

I wonder what Patty would say first.

She wouldn't say, "I'm Patty," because then I would say, "I know that already."

She wouldn't say, "I'm a dog," because I know that, too.

And she wouldn't say, "How are you? Glad to meet you," because we already met long ago, and I've known her since she was just a little ball of fur in my sleeping bag on the porch when I was little.

Maybe she would say, "I've always wanted to be a hunter."

"A hunter?" I would reply.

She would say, "Yes, all my ancestors were hunters, or we helped hunters find their prey, or we fetched it when it was downed."

My eyes would grow wide imagining long ago in England or somewhere like that, hunters in furs or big overcoats with guns or spears hunting deer in the woods, and it was a big deal because they weren't hunting for sport—they were hunting because they needed to eat.

Then I thought about Patty and me, together in the far north in the winter, bounding over the wild steppes with fire in our eyes, hungry—me with my spear and big fur boots. The winter night is closing in and

we must find shelter before the storm. We will sleep in a cave in the far north after our meal of dried meat, sleep by a fire and dream of the coming spring, Patty's paws twitching in the firelight as she runs through fields of wheat. We could be cozy together, Patty and me, hunters in the far north.

Then I wonder, What were we chasing when she was pulling me through the woods like that? It wasn't Yap Yap, that was for sure. Maybe it was that deer we saw, or a wooly mammoth or another animal from days of old. I guess I'll never know.

Picasso

by Ann M. Martin

illustrated by Olga and Aleksey Ivanov

Picasso

I am in charge of things today. Completely in charge and home alone for the first time in my life. Okay, it isn't as if my parents had some big epiphany (look it up) and realized I (a) am twelve, (b) have never been in serious trouble, and (c) got straight A's on my last report card, so therefore I can finally be considered old enough and responsible enough to stay at home alone. No. Sadly, there was no epiphany. There wasn't time for one.

What happened was that my little brother fell off his dresser, which of course he wasn't supposed to be standing on, and broke his wrist. We all heard a huge crash (my brother landed on his truck collection) and went tearing into his room—Mom, Dad, Picasso (dog), and me. And there was Anthony sitting on the floor with a bath towel tied around his shoulders, rubbing his wrist and crying, "But I'm Superman!"

No one commented on this remark. My dad untied the towel (which wouldn't have been my first response in such an emergency, but whatever), and my mom examined Anthony's wrist and announced, "I think he broke it."

Picasso and I looked on in fascination—Picasso because he had just realized that the strong smell of peanut butter in the room was coming from a sandwich Anthony had been holding at the time of his experiment and which was now lying, only partially squished, on the carpet by Anthony's bottom. I was fascinated because I want to become a doctor and this was the first actual broken bone I had ever seen.

The next thing I knew, Dad had picked up Anthony, and Mom was calling to me, "You're in charge, Delilah. Take care of things until we get back." I couldn't actually hear the last three words of that sentence, since Mom said them after she had closed the back door, but I knew what she meant.

I disposed of the squished sandwich before Picasso could eat it. Then I looked at Picasso, and he looked at me, and I said, "We're on our own."

So now here we are. At any rate, here I am.

Picasso is sort of missing.

He hasn't been missing for too long, which is the good news. In fact, he's been missing for only about ten minutes, so I am not panicking. Yet.

117

Still, I keep gazing around our backyard, trying to catch sight of some part of him: his tail, which has very long fur and waves in the breeze like a golden flag; or his head, which is on the large side and includes a nose that is half brown and a quarter white and a quarter yellow (let's face it, he isn't the most attractive dog); or any of his feet, which also have very long fur and make him look a little like a Clydesdale horse.

I don't see any parts of him or hear any of the noises he makes: woofs, yips, howls, growls, sneezes (he has allergies), or burps. Picasso is the best burper I know. Usually he waits until he has settled himself in your lap and is looking directly into your face before he lets loose with a belch that is like a fake one you'd hear on TV, that's how loud it is.

"Picasso!" I call. Then I listen for a few moments. I actually cup my hand to my ear, as if that will help me hear better. "Picasso!"

Nothing. Just the wind in the trees and

two barn swallows chattering to each other, and from far across the field, a roar, which I'm pretty sure is our neighbors' tractor starting up, so it must be mowing day.

"Picasso!" I shout. "Picasso!"

Now panic is setting in. It's amazing how quickly it can happen.

The day is very hot, and I don't feel like trekking all around our yard and into the woods beyond. The woods are on a hill. Well, so is our yard, but the hill is steeper where the woods are, and there aren't any paths through the trees, so searching is difficult. But I have to find Picasso.

I run inside, grab my sneakers, and shove them onto my feet. I always leave my sneakers pre-tied, not for speed in getting dressed, but because Picasso chews the laces if he sees them trailing across the floor. The day is not only very hot, but also very sunny, and I think that if I'm going to be outdoors for a while, I should wear sunblock and a hat. Then I think how proud my parents would be if they could see what I'm doing. It would certainly demonstrate to them that I'm responsible enough to be home alone and in charge of things.

Except for immediately losing the dog.

I run out of the house in my sneakers, sunblock glopped on my face, still pulling my ponytail through the back of my hat.

"Picasso!" I yell. "Picasso, Picasso, PICASSO!"

I lope to the edge of our property, where the woods begin, and stand by the old pear tree, looking down at our house. The house somehow seems bigger from up here, and I wonder if Picasso likes the view, since I often see him sitting in the exact spot where I'm standing now. He sits up straight and tall, the way Ms. Dooter, my science teacher (who deserves a name like that and, by the way, was the only one to give me an A- on my report card instead of a complete A), tells us to sit if we want good posture. Although I ought to point out that she is not a very effective advertisement for good posture, what

with her neck sticking out in front of her at approximately a ninety-degree angle.

I sit on a large rock for several seconds and listen again. No Picasso sounds. Then I stand on the rock and call his name a few more times. I know I'm beginning to sound a little hysterical, and I try to calm myself. After all, Picasso has only been missing for (I check my watch) twenty-one minutes.

I wonder how long my parents will be at the hospital with Anthony. Surely Picasso will return before they do. Or maybe not. Dinner, an event Picasso would never miss, is hours away. I slump a little. Then I get to my feet. "Picasso!"

I stand in the sunshine and close my eyes, which makes the insides of my lids turn bright red. I tell myself that if I call Picasso three more times and then open my eyes, I'll see him somewhere in the yard.

"Picasso! Picasso! Picasso!" I yell.

I open my eyes. Of course he's not in the yard. What was I thinking? It isn't like I'm standing on a magic rock.

Now I begin talking to myself out loud, which just goes to show you how nervous I'm getting. "Okay, Delilah," I say to myself. "You have only looked in the backyard. You have a front yard too, you know."

This thought doesn't calm me, though, because along the edge of the front yard is the driveway, and the driveway leads to the road, and the road is about the most dangerous place I can think of for a dog, especially one like Picasso, who, as appealing as he is, is not particularly bright.

I jog down the hill toward the house, and suddenly a whole list of not-too-bright things that Picasso has done begins to play in my mind. It's like I'm envisioning Picasso's bad report card.

For starters, when my family went to the shelter in search of a pet, we had intended to adopt an older dog, since older dogs have a harder time finding homes than puppies do, but we were stopped by the sight of a puppy (Picasso, obviously) who was barking at a bowl of water.

"What's he doing?" Mom asked the shelter manager.

The shelter manager's name was Brian. He shrugged. "He barks at it a lot."

"I think it's funny," I said. (I was eight.)

"Does he bark at other things?" asked my father.

"No. Just the water bowl," Brian replied.

Picasso looked at us briefly, pawed at the bowl, and barked twice more.

So we adopted him and brought him home, and I tried to come up with an explanation for his behavior. "Maybe he sees himself in the water. Maybe he's barking at his reflection," I said.

"Maybe," my father replied. And then I distinctly heard him whisper to my mother, "Picasso isn't the brightest dog."

Sadly, it was true. Picasso grew up a little and stopped barking at water bowls, and my mother even fondly pointed out to whoever would listen that he'd been housebroken far more quickly than either Anthony or I had been toilet-trained. On the other hand, we once lost track of Picasso at a state park, and while we called and shouted and frantically yelled, "Treat, Picasso!" he joined up with another family, and almost went home with them. When we caught sight of his flag tail disappearing down a path, we ran to him and hugged him and kissed him, and he gave us a look that plainly said, "Oh, were you gone? I found these nice people who had hot dogs."

"He'll do anything for a hot dog," I said later to my parents. "That's why he was going to go home with that other family."

"He's not too bright," my father whispered to my mother.

Picasso's report card is looking worse and worse, because now I also remember his problem with hiding. Every so often, Picasso tries to hide for one reason or another, usually when we have company and he doesn't want to meet anyone new. This is how a not-very-bright dog hides: with his head and front feet behind one of the dining room curtains and his tail and entire rump sticking out in full view. Once when he was hiding like this, a visiting six-year-old went shrieking into the dining room, saw Picasso's rump, and patted it, and Picasso jumped a mile because he wasn't expecting it. He was so sure he was well hidden.

So you can see why the thought of Picasso on the road is alarming. I increase my speed from a jog to a full run, and since I'm running downhill, I can barely stop myself when I reach the front yard. I actually have to grab at the side of the garage as I fly by in order to slow down. Then I stand in the middle of the yard and catch my breath and listen for Picasso sounds again. Nothing. Just the Wilsons' tractor.

"Picasso?" I call. "Picasso?"

Horrible, horrible images are creeping into my mind. I picture Picasso lying by the side of the road, unmoving. I picture a pack of coyotes taking him down. I picture someone driving along the road and luring him into a car with a piece of hot dog and selling him to a lab where unspeakable experiments are performed on him for the rest of his life, which is very short.

Picasso is plainly not in the front yard, so I run to the road and look up and down it as far as I can see, which isn't very far, since we live on a curvy, wooded country road. But at least there are no furry bodies anywhere. I don't know whether to be relieved or more frantic. Where is Picasso?

I listen to the sound of the tractor, and now I picture Mrs. Wilson riding around and around as she mows the field, and that makes me picture Cynthia Wilson behind the wheel of the Wilsons' Prius. Cynthia is seventeen and has just gotten her driver's license. I don't know much about cars—or Cynthia—but I have a feeling that Cynthia is looking for any possible excuse to get the Prius out on the road.

I jog across the Wilsons' front lawn and ring their bell. My fingers are crossed that both Cynthia and the Prius are at home. Cynthia answers the door, which is good, but I don't see a car anywhere.

"Hey, Cynthia," I say.

"Hey, Delilah. What's going on?"

This is a fair question, since there aren't any Wilsons my age and I don't have much reason to show up on their doorstep.

I think for a moment. "I heard you got your license."

Cynthia beams at me. "Yeah. I got it on Friday."

"That is so cool." (I have no idea if seventeen-year-olds say "cool.") "I can't wait until I can drive. Anyway, I was wondering . . ."

"Yeah?"

"If you could take me for a dr—" This is probably the lamest thing I've ever suggested, but the fact that Cynthia doesn't even wait until I've finished the sentence before she makes a grab for the car keys just goes to show you how eager she is to show off her new skill.

"Sure!" she exclaims. "Come on!"

In about one second, we are sitting in the Prius (which was in the garage), and about one second after that, we're nosing onto the road.

"Where do you want to go?" asks Cynthia. "Into town?"

That would be the logical destination, but I'm forced to say, "Let's just drive around here a little." There is absolutely no way I'm going to admit that the first time I was left alone and in charge I immediately lost our dog. My parents must never know about this.

"Seriously?" asks Cynthia.

"Yeah. Up and down the road and, oh, maybe out Carter Lane a little way." (Picasso and I sometimes take walks along Carter Lane, so he's familiar with the road, and he likes it because once he found part of a hamburger under a laurel bush.)

"Really? Because I'm allowed to drive into town."

"No, here is good."

So Cynthia starts speeding along our road, and I say, "Could you please slow down?"

"You don't get carsick, do you?"

I don't, but I reply, "Yeah," and look all sheepish.

Cynthia slows down, and I open my window and peer carefully at the ditch that runs along the road. I try to see into the woods too. I really want to call, "Picasso! Picasso!" but of course that would give things away.

After we've gone about a mile and a half, I say, "Okay, now could you turn around, please?"

"Here?" (We're in the middle of nowhere, but I don't think Picasso could have gotten this far already—unless he's been dognapped.) "There isn't anywhere to turn around," Cynthia points out.

Something springs to mind. All I know about driving is the stuff my mother shouts at other drivers when she gets frustrated behind the wheel. Things like "Use your signal. Your signal! You have a signal, don't you? Or am I just supposed to guess which way you're going to turn?" And "Go ahead, take up both lanes. It's fine with me. The road was made for you and you alone. Don't worry about anyone in any of the other cars." Also once I heard her shout, "Are you kidding me? You're going to make a K-turn here, in the middle of the road? Well, go ahead, take your time. No one else is in any rush. It's all about you."

"Did you learn how to make a K-turn?" I ask Cynthia now.

Cynthia brightens. "Oh! Yeah! I did. My dad says I do them really well."

"Could you show me?" I ask, trying to appear fascinated and scan the woods for Picasso at the same time.

Cynthia wrenches the wheel around, and pretty soon we're heading back the way we came and I'm checking the ditches on the other side of the road, which, thankfully, are free of dog bodies. Eventually I see the turnoff for Carter Lane, so I say, "Hey, could you demonstrate a left-hand turn? You could turn there, onto Carter."

"Sure!"

More cruising along, more searching for Picasso, more pretending to be impressed with Cynthia's driving ability, and eventually the flawless execution of another K-turn.

"Wow," I say, shaking my head. "I hope someday I'll be as good a driver as you." I gaze meaningfully at Cynthia until my eyes are drawn to a flash of tan—a moving flash of tan—through the trees a little ahead of us. I stare hard and realize that the lean haunches belong to a deer, which glances at me before crashing out of sight.

"Thank you," Cynthia replies.

She gives me a grateful smile, and I feel like a horrible person. Then I think about Picasso and feel even worse.

"You're welcome," I say anyway. "Well, you probably want to get back home. Thanks for the demonstration."

Cynthia expertly parks the Prius in the Wilsons' garage, and I lope across the road and up my driveway. I have absolutely no idea what to do next.

I fix myself some lunch. Then I sit on the front porch for a while. I remember the time Picasso poked his head through the railings to get a better view of a Pop-Tart that Anthony had accidentally dropped over the side and how he barked and sniffed and

barked some more before realizing that he couldn't pull his head back out.

"Dad! Picasso's stuck!" I had yelled into the house.

"Why am I not surprised?" replied my father, appearing at the screen door and surveying the situation.

Dad had to get his saw and remove part of one of the railings in order to free Picasso, and he wasn't happy about it.

The railing has never been repaired. I kick my foot through the space.

"Picasso!" I shout, but without any conviction.

The phone rings, and I nearly fall down the porch steps—that's how nervous I am now. I tear inside. Maybe someone has found Picasso. I don't even care if it's Cynthia Wilson and I have to confess the real purpose of the driving demonstration.

I snatch up the phone without looking at the Caller ID display. "Hello? Hello?"

"Hi, honey," says my mother's voice. "Just checking in. Everything all right?"

"Well," I say, and luckily I don't get any further before I hear a lot of static and some whooshing and crackling noises.

"Uh-oh," says Mom. "I think I'm breaking up." (*Whooooosh.*) "I'm not" (*crackle, crackle*) "be using my cell phone." (*Creeeak, crackle, crackle.*) "So we'll see you—"

The line goes dead.

"When? You'll see me when?" I cry. I shake the phone as if that will restore our connection. I'm not even sure where Mom was calling from. For all I know, they're on their way home. I imagine Dad turning onto our road two miles from here where it intersects with the highway and then screeching to a halt as Picasso saunters out of the woods.

I return to the porch, where I look toward the road and yell, "Picasso! You'd better come back right now, or you will be in very, very big trouble. And I mean it!"

Of course nothing happens. I stomp around to the backyard, stand in the middle of it, and am about to yell Picasso's name in a crabby and annoyed manner, when suddenly I remember last winter when I had the flu and Picasso spent nearly two weeks sleeping at my side. While I coughed and sneezed and burned up with fever and shivered with chills, Picasso lay peacefully on my bed. He didn't care when I tossed back the covers and started sweating, and then hugged him to me five minutes later when I was cold. He did avoid the mound of tissues that piled up when I was too weak to aim for the wastebasket, but he didn't seem to care that I had bad dreams (the kind that make you shout yourself awake) or that I smelled (a combination of sweat, cough medicine, and nose spray) or that I also had bad breath. He lay with his head on my knee and snored, day and night, until I was well.

"Picasso, where are you?" I say. I don't even bother to shout.

Now how long has he been missing? I look at my watch. Close to three hours.

This is very, very bad.

I plop down in the grass, which is starting to turn brown. It's only July third, but the last few weeks have been hot, not to mention entirely free of rain, and my parents are worrying about a drought and whether our well will go dry. I pull a fat blade of brown grass off of its stem, arrange it between my thumbs, and blow. The sound it makes is pathetic.

I'm beginning to think that I am pathetic too when something drifts to me on a little breeze and I lift my nose in the air and sniff just the way Picasso does when someone opens a package of hot dogs.

Then I realize that I actually do smell hot dogs, or something cooking on a barbecue—hot dogs, hamburgers, steak, vegetables. It's hard to tell. But this is when it dawns on me that this is Fourth of July weekend. As if to drive the point home, just as I'm getting to my feet, I hear a *pop, pop, pop* in the distance. Fireworks. I ignore the fireworks, though, and concentrate on the smell. Someone is having a cookout nearby. And if I can smell the food, then Picasso can certainly smell it (if he's still nearby). All at once, I know what I must do. I have to figure out who's having the barbecue, and then I have to crash it.

For the second time that day, I dash through our yard and down to the road. When I reach the end of our driveway, I stand there and pretend I'm Picasso. I sniff the air again. Left or right? I can't tell. Picasso would be able to follow an odor the way I follow a trail through the woods, but I have no idea which way to go. Eventually I turn right, since we have more neighbors in that direction.

I walk about half a mile, the smell goes away, and I don't hear or see anything that would indicate a party, so I turn around, walk back, pass my driveway, and continue in the other direction until I notice a mailbox with a dinky red balloon tied to it. The balloon is so small that I'm not surprised I didn't see it when I was driving around with Cynthia. I pause and listen. I hear laughter. I hear voices. I hear something clinking. At the end of the long driveway I see cars. And I definitely smell hot dogs.

This is it. I have outwitted Picasso. (Of course, he isn't very bright.)

I turn up the driveway and tiptoe along the edge of it toward a small white house with another dinky red balloon, this one fastened to a lamppost by the front door. I picture myself returning home with Picasso and making a beeline for the refrigerator, where I will add hot dogs to our shopping list. As long as we always have hot dogs in the freezer, I think, I will never be in this situation again. The only thing I'll have to do the next time he disappears is heat up a hot dog and wave it around in the yard.

I stand at the top of the driveway and try to figure out how, exactly, I will lure Picasso back to our house, considering that I haven't brought his leash with me. (Maybe *I'm* not too bright.) I could ask someone to give me a hot dog, I think, and I could feed him little bits of it as we walk home.

I tiptoe on around to the backyard, where the party is in full swing. So many thoughts about getting Picasso home are whirling around in my head that at least a full minute goes by before I realize that Picasso is nowhere in sight. He's not begging from any of the guests who are sitting in lawn chairs with plates of food in their laps; he's not under a table guiltily eating a stolen hot dog; he's not even waiting by the grill.

I skirt the yard, trying to stay out of view. I look and look and look.

The number of dogs at the party is zero.

I wonder if anyone would notice if I suddenly yelled, "Picasso!" but I really don't see the point.

He isn't here.

I walk back to the road and amble along toward my house. I don't even bother to hurry. Why should I? Picasso has been missing for hours, and Mom and Dad and Anthony will probably be home any minute.

I have blown the biggest opportunity of my entire twelve-year-old life.

I near my driveway. Across the road, I see Cynthia hosing down the Prius in the Wilsons' driveway. I wave sadly to her, and she gives me a little wave back. She must think I spend all day roaming aimlessly around our neighborhood.

Finally I turn right and walk up my own driveway. I watch my feet and notice that I have a hole in the toe of my left sneaker. I need new shoes. I'll probably have to buy them myself. After today, my parents will never give me another nickel.

I reach the top of the driveway, eyes still downcast, and this is when I trip over Picasso. He's sitting under the basketball net, tongue hanging out, giving me a doggie grin.

Picasso lets out a yip, and I let out a scream. "Picasso!"

He gets to his feet. I crouch down and

check him over thoroughly. He looks just fine.

"Where on earth were you?" I cry. I fling my arms around him and hug him, thinking how nice it is that he's hugging me back. Then I realize that Picasso isn't hugging me, he's sniffing me. I smell like barbecue.

Picasso gazes into my eyes and produces an award-winning belch.

I take him inside and direct him to his water bowl. He has a long, sloppy drink. Then I snap his leash onto his collar and lead him to the front porch. We're sitting there in a relaxed fashion when a car turns into our driveway. Mom and Dad and Anthony pile out, Anthony waving his arm around, showing off his cast like he has just had a great adventure.

"Hi, honey!" calls my mother. "How was your day?"

"Fine," I say, getting to my feet.

Picasso stands up, too, and sticks his head through the porch railings. He tries to back up and can't.

"Picasso just got stuck again," I announce.

My father closes his eyes briefly, then opens them and looks at the place where he has already removed one railing. "Why couldn't he have put his head there?" he asks, and huffs inside to find his tools.

The God of the Pond

by Valerie Hobbs

illustrated by Olga and Aleksey Ivanov

Bertha

What Emmy wanted more than anything, more than new ice skates, more than a job for her father, even more than to be tall, was to do a full flip jump. Just one perfect flip jump. Maybe even a not-so-perfect flip jump. Just as long as it was the real thing. As long as she leapt and turned in the air, landed on a back outside edge, and at least one person was there to see her do it.

Bobby. Bobby would be the perfect person. If she closed her eyes, she could see him standing right there at the edge of the pond, with his hands stuffed in his pockets, his bright blue eyes, and his cheeks pink from the cold. Emmy would leap, turn, and come down perfectly onto the ice, and Bobby would cheer and punch the air. "Yeah!"

Walking home, he might just take her hand. Perfect!

But life wasn't perfect, and Emmy knew it. She wasn't a baby. She was eleven, almost twelve. It was an actual fact that you didn't always get what you wanted, even if you asked God for it.

How many times had she prayed for new skates? A hundred?

Or you got what you asked for, but not exactly. Like praying for a dog and getting Bertha. Emmy had begged her parents for a dog for so long that she had almost given up. Then one day, one plain old, unsurprising day, her father had come home with a surprise.

Sweet, shy Bertha, whose time at the shelter had almost run out. Bertha, with her sad eyes and long, wet doggie kisses. Bertha, who wriggled all over with love.

Bertha, the chicken killer. Bertha, the dog no fence could keep in.

If life were perfect, Bobby would have the perfect grandfather, not Old Man Brennan. Mean Old Man Brennan with his hundreds of chickens.

Just this morning, she had opened the front door and there he had been.

"This your mutt?" he'd said.

Emmy had nodded.

Old Man Brennan had handed her the rope he'd tied to Bertha's collar.

"He got another one of my chickens," he'd said. "And if I find him after my chickens again, he's a dead dog." His words had come out in great white puffs.

Under his left arm, pointed down, was a gun with two long barrels.

"She," said Emmy. Bertha had pushed her

wet nose into Emmy's hand. Her skinny tail slapped against Emmy's legs.

Mr. Brennan's red face had creased up in a frown. "Are you sassing me, young lady?"

"No, sir."

"You tell your folks what I said. One more chicken, no more dog."

"Yes, sir," said Emmy.

Old Man Brennan had turned away, and Emmy quietly closed the door.

Her heart was beating as hard as Bertha's tail.

She shook her finger at Bertha. "You're a bad girl, Bertha," she'd said.

Bertha had done her little yip-yip. What's wrong? What's all the fuss about?

But Bertha knew. She had been grounded for a month, ever since she'd come home covered with feathers.

"No chickens. Do you understand?" Emmy had said.

Bertha had cocked her head, as if trying her best to do what Emmy said: understand.

"Did you hear me? NO CHICKENS."

Bertha had pawed Emmy's foot and wriggled her skinny backside. She smiled like no dog Emmy had ever seen. Pet me, pet me. I'm your best friend.

Emmy's mother had come out of the bathroom smelling like lemon, her favorite shower gel. "Who was that?"

Emmy's pulses were all on alarm. "Just the paper guy." She had not been able to look her mother in the eye, so she'd patted Bertha instead.

"Don't let Bertha out," said her mother.

"I didn't do it!" said Emmy. "It was Dad!"

Emmy had put on her down jacket, hat, and gloves, and grabbed up her ice skates. "I'm going skating," she said. "Bertha's coming with me."

"Be careful," her mother said, which was what she always said, even in the dead of winter when the ice was rock hard.

Bertha had submitted to the muzzle and

the leash, her eyes dark and tragic. *Trust me*, her eyes said, even though she couldn't be trusted and probably knew it.

Bertha had pulled Emmy up the road that had been cleared the week before. Little mounds of crunchy, sooty snow lay along the side. It had been a long, cold winter with plenty of good days for skating, and Emmy had finally learned to do a half flip. Now, at winter's end, she was working on the full. If she did just one, she'd be the only kid besides Sara Stewart to do that trick. Sara actually did a triple once, but she was sixteen, a whole five years older than Emmy.

Emmy stood at the top of the hill, looking down at Brennan's Pond.

The boys had been busy with their brooms, and the ice was half cleared.

No Bobby.

Emmy's heart fell. She tried to tell herself that the day wasn't ruined, but it was. It had started out ruined.

Emmy tied Bertha's leash to a tree and took off her muzzle. Bertha whined and slapped her tail against the tree. Then she turned three times and plopped down on a patch of dirt to sulk.

Every inch of ice was scarred over with skate marks. Emmy stepped onto "the girls' side" and glided off. Turning, she looked back across the ice at Bertha, who was on her feet again.

Sara Stewart and a couple of her friends were coming down from the road, their skates slung around their necks. They all wore tights that looked brand-new and short skirts.

Emmy's tights had a hole in the knee from when she had taken a particularly bad fall, but her skirt almost hid it. She was never going to grow. All her life she would be four feet six inches, a shrimp.

Turning lazy circles, Emmy watched Sara

step onto the ice in her snow boots and jump a few times, then go a little farther out and do the same thing. She shook her head and went back to her friends. Emmy heard them shout, "The ice is no good!" But the boys waved them off and kept skating.

Emmy began skating back. She listened, as she hadn't earlier, for the ominous sound of ice breaking up. But the boys were still skating, slamming the puck and each other as if nothing in the world mattered but making a goal. She skated back to shore.

Bertha was busy strangling herself. She had run round and round the tree until her leash was wound tight. Emmy had a hard time convincing her that she had to go back the other way, and an even harder time trying to get her muzzle back on. Why the muzzle when poor old Bertha was on her leash? Emmy's mother was just being extra cautious, as usual.

Her father never was. He knew better than to let Bertha out without her muzzle, but he did it anyway. "What's a chicken or two?" he'd said the first time Bertha came home with feathers.

But her father had not seen Old Man Brennan standing on the porch this morning with a shotgun.

She was going to have to tell her parents.

But she couldn't. If she did, her mother would say it was "time." Time to find Bertha a good home somewhere else, a place where there were no chickens.

But she had to. If she didn't, her father would let Bertha out tomorrow, and Old Man Brennan would shoot her. Which was worse than Bertha living somewhere else, or even the shelter. Worse than anything Emmy could imagine.

All afternoon, as Emmy worked on an art project and Bertha paced back and forth behind the door, she thought about how to tell her parents.

At dinner, she couldn't eat. Every bite felt like a hockey puck going down her throat.

At last, she forced herself to say, "Um, this morning?"

Bertha gave a little groan, as if she knew what was coming.

Her mother smiled encouragingly. "Yes?"

Her father looked up from his potatoes.

"I meant to tell you this morning, only—"

Her mother's eyebrows came together. "Only what?"

"Well . . . the snow and all . . . and it is Saturday. . . ."

Which had nothing to do with anything.

Her mother tilted her head and did her little mother frown. "And?"

"Mom. Dad. Bertha killed another chicken."

"No!" said her mother.

"Huh," said her father, setting his fork down.

"Mr. Brennan brought her home on a rope, and he had this gun and—"

"What?" Her mother stood. Pushing back her chair, she stepped on Bertha's paw. Bertha yelped like she'd been shot. "I will not have guns in my house. What was that man thinking of! Guns around children!"

"Calm down, Alice," Emmy's father said.

"He wasn't actually in the house," said Emmy. "He was on the porch the whole time."

Her mother was wringing the life out of a dish towel. "As if that makes one bit of difference!" She grimaced and made up her mind. "It's time for Bertha to go," she said.

"No!" cried Emmy.

Her mother brushed the hair back from Emmy's face. "I'm sorry, honey."

Emmy jumped up and ran to her room. Slamming the door, she threw herself on her bed and cried until she made herself sick. It wasn't Bertha's fault. She loved to chase chickens the way Emmy loved to skate. It was in her blood.

It was all her father's fault. Why couldn't he just remember to muzzle Bertha?

Was it the war? The war in Iraq was the reason for everything else: why he couldn't sleep or keep a job, why he smoked, why his mind drifted off in the middle of a conversation.

So maybe it wasn't his fault. It was the war's fault. Or the president's fault. But Bertha could die, no matter whose fault it was.

Mr. Brennan's fault. He was the one with the stupid chickens. And the gun.

She had to help her father remember. When her stomach finally settled, she got up and dug out her felt pens. On two big pieces of paper, in giant red letters, she wrote REMEMBER THE MUZZLE.

Beneath the words, she drew Bertha with big, sad eyes. The first Bertha looked like a raccoon; the second one was a little better. She taped the signs next to the front and back doors, where her father couldn't miss seeing them. Before turning in, she set her alarm clock. At five A.M., she would get up, muzzle Bertha, and let her out. That would be her job from now on.

She would tell her father about the new plan, but he'd probably just forget.

She awoke to the sound of rain—4:40. She turned off her alarm and yawned. She closed her eyes. In five minutes she would get up and let Bertha out.

When she awoke again, the rain had stopped—6:10.

Bertha! She leapt out of bed and raced to the living room.

There was Bertha, asleep on her blanket. Her father was standing at the window, looking out, steam rising from his World's Greatest Dad coffee mug. According to him, a day could not begin without coffee.

"Did you let Bertha out, Daddy?"

"Hmmmm?"

"Bertha. Does she need to go out?"

Her father turned and smiled, as if he'd just woken up. "Good morning, cookie. You're up early."

Emmy joined him at the window. "It's stopped raining. Good."

"That's the end of the skating for this year," he said. He put his arm around Emmy, giving her a sideways squeeze.

Her heart tumbled downhill. One more day on the ice, and she'd have her flip jump. She just knew it.

They ate their Cheerios together. Then her father went out to his garage workshop, and she went outside. It was cold. Cold enough.

Well, maybe not cold enough. But cold. The sky was a frozen gray. Her breath came out white. A little voice inside told her that this would be her last chance, that she had to hurry.

She went back inside, dressed, and gathered up her skates. It was Sunday, and her mother was sleeping in.

Bertha was sleeping in, too. Was she sick? Emmy felt her nose. Bertha opened one eye, banged her tail against the wall, and went back to sleep. Emmy crept out the door.

The sun was just coming up, a soft orange smudge behind the leafless trees. Emmy hurried up the wet road. The sooner she got to the pond, the better. The air would warm up as the day went on, and the ice would begin to melt.

But for now, there was time. There had to be. Just one quick flip. One perfect, even not-so-perfect flip.

Rainwater glazed the pond. It had never looked so beautiful or so still, and Emmy had it all to herself. Stepping out onto the ice, she was Emily Hughes at Nationals, ready for her free skate. She glided off. Not a sound but the scritch and scratch of her blades. She would skate to the other side of the pond and back. By then, she would be warmed up. By then, Bobby might be coming down the hill and she would do her first ever flip jump.

On the pond's far end, water was seeping up through the ice. Water?

Emmy stopped. Her breath came short. She turned and began skating back fast to where the ice was safe.

She felt it before she knew exactly what was happening, a sickening lurch in the pit of her stomach as the ice cracked and began to give. Then, ever so slowly, as if it had all the time in the world, the black water rose up through the sinking floor and took her down.

Under the freezing, dark water Emmy thrashed in all directions, through her own bubbles, not knowing which way was up and out. Branches underwater, like withered arms, snagged her sleeve. But then her skates touched on something, just the tips of their blades, and she gave one huge push upward.

She broke through the surface, gasping, screaming. "Help! Help, somebody!"

Her jaw ached, her teeth began to chatter like a windup toy. She clung to a shelf of ice, afraid to look down. All that black water. Every prayer she ever knew rose to her lips.

If she weren't so cold, she could believe she was dreaming. She could wake herself out of this.

How had she let herself believe that a flip jump was worth more than her life?

"Help! Somebody, help!"

From the other side of the pond came a

familiar bark, and Bertha came racing across the ice, a brown blur, slipping and sliding, falling and getting back up, heading straight for Emmy.

"No, Bertha! Go back! You'll fall through!" But Bertha was determined. As the ice cracked around them, Bertha tugged on Emmy's sleeve with all thirty pounds of her might. She couldn't budge Emmy, who had begun to wail.

"Get help, Bertha," she begged. Bertha whined and pulled.

Someone was coming down the hill, a moving black shadow.

"Help!" cried Emmy through frozen lips. Her voice cracked. She was turning to ice. "Help me!"

Old Man Brennan stopped perfectly still at the edge of the pond, a black cutout silhouette stuck onto white paper. He looked down then, as if he'd lost something. Then he turned and went back up the way he had come. Bertha took off after him. Catching

up, she ran circles around his legs, barking and barking.

Emmy tried again to hoist herself out, but the ice broke under her weight. She thrashed in the water until she could grab on again.

Was this the way it happened? Was this the way she would die? Would Old Man Brennan let her freeze to death because of a couple of chickens?

Then she saw him coming back, trudging down the hill with his shotgun. Where was Bertha? Had he shot her? Was he going to shoot Emmy, too?

Was he crazy?

But there was Bertha, racing down the hill, past Old Man Brennan and onto the ice. She grabbed onto Emmy's sleeve again and, lowering her haunches, began to pull.

Old Man Brennan made his way toward them, slowly, carefully, testing each step, his face hidden in the collar of his jacket. A loose snap on his huge black boots rattled.

Kneeling, he began crawling on his hands and knees across the ice. He pushed the big barrel of the gun toward her. His eyes, shadowed under the brim of his hat, looked almost afraid. When the pipe—not a shotgun!—reached her, Emmy grabbed on like a fish biting bait.

Slowly, carefully, Old Man Brennan pulled Emmy out and over the ice. Then she was sitting on her bottom, curled up with her arms around her soaked tights and wailing like a wet baby while Bertha licked her face.

"Careful, now," said Old Man Brennan, helping Emmy to her feet. With his hands on her shoulders, he guided her back over the ice.

When Bertha saw that Emmy was safe, she took off, skidding and slipping across the ice and into the woods.

Old Man Brennan wrapped his jacket around Emmy and lifted her into his arms. "We've got to get you home," he said.

"Bertha's gone after your chickens," Emmy mumbled through Popsicle lips.

It was only fair to tell him.

"You almost lost your life, young lady," he said.

By the end of February, the ice was melting fast, and by March, it was gone. Emmy went to the pond to sit and think, no matter the season. She turned twelve in March, and there was so much to think about when you were twelve. She had grown almost an inch. There was hope. Sometimes she was by herself, and sometimes Bobby came down the hill and sat beside her on the log. They talked about school, their teachers, friends and family, the usual things.

They both missed skating and talked about his dreams of being on the Rangers and hers of being in the Olympics. Emmy hadn't done a flip jump after all, but she wasn't giving up hope. Some things took time, and flips were one of those things.

"How come your grandfather doesn't come down to the pond anymore?" said Emmy on one long and lazy afternoon, happy that she and Bobby had the pond to themselves.

"No ice," said Bobby. When he looked

over at her, Emmy saw a change in him. It was as if he'd thought of something he didn't like to remember. "When he was twelve, his little sister fell through the ice and drowned."

A chill ran through Emmy. "She drowned right here? In this pond?"

"Right here," he said. They both looked out at the greenish-black water as if they could see it happening. "My grandpa tried to pull her out, but he couldn't."

"So he watches you?"

"Sometimes he watches even when I'm not there. He's like the god of the pond."

Bertha lay with her muzzled snout on the log, right between them, as if she'd been sent by Emmy's mother to keep them apart.

"Your grandpa thinks I'm an idiot, right?"

"He says you're too brave for your own good. But I can tell that he likes you." Bobby patted Bertha, who was clearly in love with him. "At least Bertha hasn't killed any more chickens."

At the mention of her name, Bertha's tail thumped the ground.

"I put a sign on my dad's Mr. Coffee machine," said Emmy. "Now he never forgets."

By the middle of May, Brennan's Pond was warm enough to wade in, but the bottom was thick with mud that sucked you down, and nobody ever swam in it. There were cattails all along one side, leaves on the trees, birds that settled in the branches at dusk and gossiped about their day, frogs that blinked their big wise eyes. By August, Bobby and Emmy were holding hands, unless Bertha was there to nudge them apart.

Bertha kept catching chickens, but only in her dreams. Emmy could tell by her

scrambling feet and the smile on her face as she slept.

On December 21, the official start of winter, Emmy did a full, only-a-little-crooked, almost-perfect flip jump, and Bertha and Bobby and the whole hockey crew were there to see it happen.

Trail Magic

by Margarita Engle

illustrated by Olga and Aleksey Ivanov

Gabe

In my other life there were pit bulls.
The puppies weren't born vicious,
but Mom taught them how to bite,
turning meanness into money,
until she got caught.

Now I live in a high mountain cabin
with my brave forest ranger uncle,

and I only see Mom on visiting days,
when the heavy gate of a lowland prison
slides shut behind me, making me feel small
and trapped.

I'm not small—I'm almost twelve, the
    tallest boy
in my tiny, three-room mountain school.
Living in the forest feels like time travel.
Tío reminds me of heroes in ancient stories,
fearless people who knew how to fly,
talk to animals, and face any danger
without sinking into the huge
loneliness
of nightmares.

Tío takes me bird-watching and stargazing
in places without any traffic or lights.
He shows me how to survive lightning
    storms
and where to find roots and berries.
He patrols the Pacific Crest Trail,
where hikers from all over the world

walk thousands of miles, just to find
peace and quiet, luxuries I never imagined
in my old life of rage and pain.
Peace and quiet feel like a mysterious
sort of medicine.

Tío promises that someday I'll feel brave,
but I swear it isn't true.
I'm a coward.
I'm even scared of falling asleep.
I'm scared of dreams.

When my uncle is out making his rounds,
I'm alone in the cabin with his friendly
search-and-rescue dog, a shelter mutt
with the glow of a golden retriever,
the genius of a border collie,
and the name of a boy: Gabe.
Tío thinks dogs deserve human names
to remind us that they're alive,
with real feelings, like joy and pain.

Tío and Gabe and I are a team.
We serve hamburgers and wild berry pies

PACIFIC
CREST
TRAIL

to backpackers who visit our cabin.
The hikers come from places like Iceland,
    Japan,
and Australia, talking with exotic accents
as they tell stories about other mountains
they've hiked—the Andes, the Alps, the
    Himalayas.
Listening to their adventures,
I imagine the size of the world.
No wonder I feel small.

Backpackers headed all the way from
    Canada
to Mexico are called thru-hikers.
They leave their everyday lives behind,
choosing trail names like Wolf, Wild Man,
Explorer, or Skywalker.
I imagine those trail names must help
the hikers feel free and heroic,
but when they ask me what trail name
I'd choose if I was old enough to walk
all over the world, I can't even begin
to imagine being that brave.

Strangely, I'm not afraid of dogs.
You'd think I would be, after all the fights
I've seen, all the growling I've heard.

Thru-hikers call my uncle a trail angel,
meaning a stranger who spreads trail magic,
which is any unexpected act of kindness,
like sharing food or finding the lost.
The Pacific Crest Trail passes through places
with names like Desolation, where
    exhausted hikers
sometimes lose their way.

That's when Gabe's amazing nose
goes into action, sniffing like crazy,
twitching so hard I can hear the air
    popping
in and out of his nostrils.

Dogs think work and fun
are exactly the same thing.
Gabe gets bouncy and excited,
but he's serious too, as if he understands

that search and rescue is a life-or-death
    game
of hide-and-seek.

Life-or-death games are all I knew
back in my old life, when I had to take care
of dogs that could have killed me.

Mountain chores are safe and easy.
All I have to do is weed the vegetable
    garden,
stack firewood, chop fruit for pies, and hide
way out in the forest, so Gabe can practice
finding a lost person.

When a wilderness area dog like Gabe is
    searching,
he runs back and forth in a big zigzag
    pattern,
sniffing the air until he finds my scent.
Then he turns and races back to alert Tío,
who praises him and tosses a squeaky toy.
Gabe's reward for winning at hide-and-seek

is playing fetch, only he can't work alone.
He needs guidance.
Without Tío's instructions,
Gabe would be as mixed up and confused
as a boy raised by pit bulls.
On the other hand, once Gabe understands
what he's supposed to do,
he moves like a shooting star,
a fiery streak of pure energy!

Once the life-or-death game
of hide-and-seek is finally over,
it's time to rest.

At night in the cabin, Gabe curls up
beside me, and I listen to his breath.
The unworried rhythm is like music,
helping me relax and forget to be scared
of memory-dreams that make the past
still seem real.

When Gabe dreams, his eyelids flicker,
and I imagine that I can see his thoughts.

Before the shelter, he must have been lonely,
just a puppy lost on a mountain road,
hoping to be found and rescued.
Now he finds and rescues lost people.
Some things in life actually do make sense.
So why can't I ever imagine my mom's
    thoughts?
The dogfights were ugly and noisy.
I didn't know how to make the meanness
    stop.
Drunk men came to bet money—scary men,
betting on scary dogs, but the next morning,
I had to feed those dogs and patch their
    wounds.
I took them for long, tail-wagging walks,
just like any other boy who had never
heard snarls or touched scars.

Gabe wakes me up out of the memories.
We stop dreaming, we get up, move around,
set ourselves free of the past.
The weather is clear and warm.
The forest is alive with clean smells,

pine, incense cedar, and wildness.
It's Saturday, no school, and Tío is already
out in the woods, working weekends
because it's just past summer, the busy
    season,
when even the most remote campgrounds
are crowded.

I take Gabe out for a run, feed him,
and heat up some leftover pie for myself.
There's no Internet or cell phone
    reception
up here, but I have a two-way radio
for checking in to let my uncle know I'm
    fine.
The problem is, today he's patrolling
on such a remote peak that even my radio
won't reach him.

I'm not fine.
Memory-dreams have a way of leaving
a bitter aftertaste, like strong medicine.
To get away from the creeping sadness,
I take my radio out to the garden,

where I can pretend Tío is close.
I pretend the thorny weeds
are alien invaders and I'm a superhero,
chasing them back to their own planet.

Gabe tries to help, but he digs up
Tío's prize heirloom tomato plants,
along with the giant alpine dandelions.
So I stop hoeing and just blow a bunch
of dandelion fluff up into the sky.
It makes me feel babyish with hope,
but I have to admit I love to watch
all those wispy wishes twirl and rise.

A call comes in on the radio,
but it's not my uncle—it's a search,
a real search, not just practice.
There's a lost child, a little boy
who wandered away from a campsite.
What were the grown-ups doing?
How could they fail to pay attention?
Gabe stares up at me with eager wolf eyes.
He recognizes the radio's automated voice
calling for volunteers to join the search.

He knows words like *deploy* and *urgent*.
Gabe is just as much of a natural-born trail
    angel
as my uncle—I'm the only one who doesn't
    know
how to help.

Vermilion, that's where the radio tells
searchers to meet and be deployed,
sent out to various portions of the area
where the lost boy might be found.
Vermilion isn't too far. I could make it
on the ATV, a super-cool all-terrain vehicle
that looks like a golf cart and drives
like a motorbike.

I'm not supposed to take the ATV
past the driveway, but I do know how,
and this is an emergency, hide-and-seek,
life or death.

Tío would disapprove.
Or would he?

Isn't he the one who always
insists that I can be brave?
I could do it, with Gabe's help
I could find that little lost kid.
I'd be a hero.
I'd be a trail angel,
filled with magic.

Gabe's eyes urge me to go, go, go!
He sits beside me on the ATV while I talk,
reminding him that we can't really search
because I don't have the CPR training
or any of the dog-handling skills Tío has
    studied
and mastered, day after day, year after year.
We'll just watch.
We'll just be heroic observers.
We start gliding, slowly at first, then faster,
until we're on a narrow dirt road,
and then we've reached Vermilion,
a lively rest stop where two trails meet
and all the thru-hikers have to take a ferry
across Edison Lake.

There are dozens of people milling around,
some on horseback, leading pack mules
and llamas loaded with bundles.
I feel like I've landed in a faraway country
where animals are still a huge part
of daily life.

Gabe is crazy with excitement.
I hold on to his leash, so we can hang out
near a table where sheriffs are giving
instructions to all sorts of search-and-rescue
volunteers—mounted posses, dog teams,
ATV teams, and plenty of ground
     pounders,
people on foot who just walk around
trying to spot footprints in meadow grass
or pine needles, or on the mud
of slippery creek banks.

When Gabe bumps my leg with his nose,
I'm sure I can hear his thoughts.
Go, go, go, find, find, find!
But he isn't wearing his orange vest

with SEARCH DOG written on the sides,
and I'm not carrying a GPS for mapping
the area of interest, a circle that grows wider
and wider as minutes pass.
What if the little boy is still wandering
farther and farther, getting more and more
lonely and lost?

I try calling my uncle on the radio,
just in case he might be close enough.
Nothing.
Why did Tío choose this crazy day
to leave me alone without contact,
without any way to communicate
and ask him for help?
I recognize the dogs and handlers,
but they're too busy to notice me.
The handlers are volunteers, but they wear
official-looking uniforms, and they carry
heavy backpacks filled with emergency gear,
in case the search goes on overnight.
They have first aid supplies and space
    blankets,

food, water, matches. . . .
All I have is my uncle's dog.
If I found a lost, scared little boy,
I wouldn't be much use.
I'd be helpless,
not heroic.

Thru-hikers weave in and out of the crowd
of searchers, some talking English,
others chattering in their own languages.
There's a chaplain in a sheriff's uniform,
praying with people who must be the lost
    boy's
desperate, anxious, guilty family.
I feel like I've gone traveling to some
    faraway,
scary planet, even though I'm just a few
    miles
from the safe, quiet cabin.

Next thing I know, I really have gone away.
I don't know if it's courage or foolishness.
All I know is I want to help, I have to try.

Gabe whines beside me on the seat of the
   ATV
as I race it out onto a little side trail
that none of the searchers have reached yet.
Pretty soon, we've left the crowd behind.
We're in unfamiliar country, seeing plenty
of tracks, but none of them are human.

I park in a meadow, get off, and turn Gabe
   loose.
He goes into his zigzag search pattern,
expecting me to guide him
to the right areas, but all I can do is hope.
I have no idea where to search.
I don't know the right commands.
I can't read Gabe's movements.
It's like I'm illiterate in the mysterious
language of dogs.

We pass the musky scent of a bear den.
There are piles of colorful bear scat,
red poop next to Manzanita bushes,
blue piles near ripe elderberries.

I don't know what I was thinking.
This isn't a dog movie where the kid
turns into a hero because his puppy
knows the way.

Gabe is already frustrated.
He wants me to tell him what to do.
He knows his job, but I don't know mine.
So I get on the radio and try to call Tío.
That's when I find out the battery has died.
Now I'm scared beyond belief.
So is Gabe.
He smells my fear and makes it his own.
We climb back onto the ATV, but as soon
as I try to spin a U-turn and head home,
we flip over, and even though we're both
alive, we're bruised and scratched,
and the ATV is stuck upside down
in soft sand.
I feel as panicky
as I used to when the pit bulls
were fighting to entertain
human bullies.

What have I done?
How could I be so selfish?
Gabe is worried and whiny,
and his fear is my fault.
Worst of all, we aren't any use
when it comes to my far-fetched
daydream of becoming heroic
by helping
that lost little kid.

We have to walk now.
It's farther than I thought.
Gabe is thirsty, so we find a stream,
but once we've branched away from our trail,
I can't find my way back.
Gabe's sense of smell could lead us,
but I don't know how to tell him
what we need.
I make up my mind
to take dog training classes,
and pay more attention
to my surroundings,
and visit Mom more often,

now that I know
what it feels like
to do something dumb
and mess up.

If you get lost in the woods,
you're supposed to stay in one place
and wait to be found, but most people
just slide into a deeper and deeper panic,
and that's how I feel now, crazy with fear,
even though fear makes everything
worse, a lot worse. . . .

Gabe is hungry.
He chases a dragonfly, but he can't catch it,
and even though I know he loves berries,
I'm afraid to go near bear-scented bushes,
so we just nibble a few round, bitter leaves
of miner's lettuce, both of us wishing
for Tío's burgers and pie.

A helicopter whirs far overhead,
but I don't have a signal mirror,
and I know they're looking

for the other lost boy.
No one knows that I'm gone yet.
No one's searching for me.

Later, after I've run in circles
and confused Gabe, the cloudy truth
starts to get clear.

We'll be out overnight.
It's already twilight.
If I had a trash bag, I could fill it
with pine needles to make a sleeping bag.
If I had a fish hook . . .
If I knew how to find my way
by following stars . . .
If I had common sense . . .

Gabe keeps one side of me warm.
Looking up, beyond windblown trees,
we watch the half moon, wondering
what we'll do if the weather turns stormy,
if lightning strikes, if Tío loses custody
because I made him seem
like an irresponsible foster parent. . . .

Gabe is the first one to hear the shriek.
It sounds like a cross between a huge bird
and an eerie ghost in an old horror movie.
I know what it is, because my uncle
has described it a million times.
A mountain lion.
Or La Llorona, a mythical woman
who screams because she can't
find her children.
Tío says you can't tell mountain lions
and the Weeping Woman apart
just by sound, you have to see tracks,
but there's no way I'm getting up
to follow eerie moonlit footprints.

What would I do if I actually spotted
a mountain lion, anyway?
Tío has told me, over and over:
stand tall, wave a branch, be enormous,
never crouch or run, don't look like prey.

Gabe is silent.
He's holding his breath.

He knows the sound of a predator.
Or a mythical being.
He probably smells whatever it is.
He could tell me which direction to go
if running away was an option.
We lie still.
We don't breathe.
I wonder if Gabe can hear my thoughts
the way I imagine that I can hear his.

Somehow, we survive until morning.
Then we walk over rocks, between shrubs,
and past purple bear scat, even though I
    know
we should stay still, be patient, wait. . . .
By now there must be two searches,
one for a boy too young to know better
and one for a big boy who got careless.
Tío must be going crazy.
I'll be grounded forever, if I even get to stay
and live with him until college, like we'd
    planned.
Forestry, that's what I was going to study

if I'd been smart enough to stay out of
    trouble.

Gabe is up and gone.
I try to follow, but he races so fast
that I trip and fall, then scramble back up,
wishing, wishing, GIANT wishing
that I'd followed the rules.
A weight knocks me down,
swipes my breath, closes my eyes,
and when I open them, all I can see
is the dusky gold of a mountain lion's coat.
But it's Gabe, slamming against me,
alerting me, letting me know he's won
the life-or-death hide-and-seek game.
I smile.
I walk calmly.

There he is, the little boy, sound asleep,
tucked way under a twisted, wind-stunted
scrap of splintered pine tree.
No one could have spotted him
from a helicopter.

Without Gabe, I would have walked
right past him and seen nothing.
Gabe's nose found him.
Now it's up to me to carry him
out into the open, yell, wave my shirt,
stay in one place, and wait to be found.

Orange vests.
Four-legged trail angels.
It happens just like it's supposed to.
Dogs find us, people rescue us,
the little boy's mom cries, thanks me,
and tells me she loves me,
while Tío hugs me and admits
that he's furious.

The next few days aren't easy,
but nobody sends me away.
The cabin is crowded with thru-hikers
from Belgium, France, and New Zealand,
everyone calling me Wizard.
The trail name sticks, and even though I
    know
I'm not really a trail magician yet,

at least I do have hope.
Maybe I'll make it to college after all,
study forestry, and find some way
to repay my uncle for his trust.

When Mom gets out of prison,
I plan to ask Tío to invite her
up to the cabin to meet Gabe.
Together, Gabe and I can help her
clear up a few cloudy truths
about brave dogs
and scared boys.

Things People Can't See

by Matt de la Peña

illustrated by Olga and Aleksey Ivanov

Peanut

The day after Chico lost his dog, Peanut, he was beaten in a fight at school.

At least the fight part was something he could've predicted. Chico was new at the private junior high on the hill. He was the scholarship kid who got bused in every morning from the wrong side of the freeway. The outsider whose old man worked the endless flower fields behind Home Depot.

"See all them poinsettias?" his dad had just told him in Spanish at parent-teacher night. He was motioning toward the dense row of Christmas-colored flowers circling the two-story, brick library.

Chico nodded as they walked the wide path that cut through the heart of his new school.

"Every single one of 'em, boy. I raised it up from a tiny little seed. Like a pea in the palm of your hand."

Chico nodded some more, but in truth he wasn't thinking of pea-sized seeds or greenhouse-grown poinsettias. Nah, he was too busy watching his new classmates watch him and his dad.

He was seeing, for the first time, how they saw him.

And he felt ashamed.

The Fight

Calling it a fight, actually, was a bit of a stretch. More like Chico acted a fool and got jumped.

He was walking across the field on his way to first period, minding his own, reminiscing about Peanut, when he spotted a pack of kids following him with their eyes.

"Hey!" one of them yelled.

Chico kept walking.

"New dude!" another voice called out.

Chico gritted his teeth.

He was in no mood. He'd just lost his dog, man. His closest friend in the world. And he was working on zero sleep. He'd spent half the previous night stalking the neighborhood, calling Peanut's name, whistling, peeking over backyard fences. The remaining hours were spent crying into his pillow like a punk little kid.

"That's rude, bro!" he heard another voice yell. "People are trying to talk to you!"

Chico slowed to a stop, imagining the

inside of these rich kids' heads. To them he was a fly in the lemonade. A smudge on the screen of a brand-new laptop. He was their gardener. Their cleaning lady. The smiling busboy who collected dirty plates at their fancy restaurants.

In other words, Chico told himself, he was nobody.

He spun around quick with a chip on his shoulder. Marched toward the pack with clenched fists, shouting, "Who you talking to?"

The pack seemed caught off guard.

"Slow down," a guy named Gabe said, raising his hands and backing up.

"What's your problem?" another kid said.

"Maybe *you're* my problem," Chico told him.

They all looked at each other.

A few smiled.

Like Chico was funny.

Like Chico attending the school on the hill was a big joke.

That's when David Winters, Mr. Popularity, said, "Why the attitude, compadre? We just wanted to ask you a question."

Chico took another step forward. "What'd you just call me?"

There were six or seven of them. All dudes. All staring at him. Daring him.

One guy got off his beach cruiser and let it fall to the grass.

"You heard me," David said, smiling.

"You heard the man," another guy chimed in.

Then David said it again: "Compadre."

None of the fragmented thoughts flashing through Chico's mind told him to walk away. Nah, he'd seen the way they looked at him at parent-teacher night. Looked at his old man. They thought they were better.

And worse than that, a tiny part of Chico thought they were right.

That's the part that swung a closed fist at the closest kid. David Winters. Blasted him in the cheek.

David stumbled backward but didn't go down. He reached for his face. Checked fingers for blood that wasn't there.

Chico stepped forward, connected again. This time in the gut. David went down on one knee. When he looked up at Chico, his eyes seemed innocent.

A second of silence followed the body blow. It felt like minutes. Everybody looking at each other, trying to process, trying to imagine what was happening, Chico's chest going in and out and in and out, his mind unable to stick with one thought.

Then they were on him.

All seven of them.

Gabe held his arms back as David shoved his face, smacked him in the side of the head, in the ribs. Somebody kicked out Chico's legs, sent him sprawling to the ground. The pack's weight crushing down on him. Tweaking his neck. Making it impossible to breathe.

Under the pile, in the darkness, Chico secretly begged for more.

He knew something these rich kids didn't.

He deserved this beatdown.

For losing his dog. For coming to this private school in the first place.

Go on! he screamed inside his head. *Hit me, punk! Do it!*

But the barrage of flying fists had already stopped. The weight had lifted. He could breathe again.

Chico leapt to his feet, ready for more. But instead of locking eyes with Gabe and David Winters and everybody he was fighting, he found two male teachers grabbing arms and pushing people away.

"All right," the one with the clipboard said. "Somebody's gonna tell me what happened. Otherwise I march every single one of you to Principal Van Buren's office."

"What's it gonna be?" the whistle teacher said. "Who started it?"

"We need answers, gentlemen."

Without thinking, Chico stepped forward. Said it was him.

What did he care?

Maybe they'd do everybody a favor and kick him out of school. Send him back where he belonged, the public junior high down the street from the greenhouses.

With his friends.

With people like him.

The Inheritance

When Chico's grandmother, on his mom's side, passed she left him two things:

A bond for his education.

And her dog, Peanut.

She left the bond because she believed a

kid with grades like Chico's should be able to attend the best school around. From her hospital bed she arranged for him to take the pre SAT, hoping he might score high enough to be admitted to the private school on the hill.

Not only did Chico score high enough to get in, his score was so freakishly high they offered him a full scholarship through high school.

"What if I don't wanna go?" Chico asked his old man on the bus ride home from his grandma's cremation.

"Oh, you're going," his dad answered in Spanish.

All their conversations went like this. Chico spoke English, and his old man would answer in Spanish. They could both speak the other's first language, but they were embarrassed by clumsy accents.

"What about my friends?" Chico said.

"Make new ones."

"What about the money, then?"

"We'll save it for your college."

Chico rolled his eyes. He was pissed.

But he was something else, too. Something he couldn't put his finger on.

Minutes passed. The bus lurched forward and stopped, lurched forward and stopped.

Finally his old man cleared his throat, said, "I made a promise to that woman, Chico. I ain't going back on it just 'cause I got a kid who's *un miedica*."

"I ain't scared," Chico shot back.

His dad looked at him, grinning.

Chico shook his head and turned to look out the window. The poor side of the freeway flashing past. Boarded storefronts and tagged windows, old Mexican men pushing carts overflowing with bottles and cans and dirty blankets.

He glanced at his dad on the sly. Guy never made it passed sixth grade, but he was right. That was the exact feeling Chico couldn't name.

He was scared.

A month later, as Chico walked onto campus for the first time, he would remember the name his old man had called him on the bus that day. Scaredy cat. Because even though he was now an official student at the school on the hill, he still felt like an imposter. Like at any second security would come barreling around the corner in their golf carts, tackling him onto the wet lawn, pulling their canisters of mace.

Peanut

Nothing really changed when Chico's grandma left him her old dog. Peanut had already been living with them for two years, since his grandma first found out she was sick.

Chico's dad wasn't too excited with the arrangement. Peanut dug holes in their tiny backyard. And dog food, even the generic kind, he constantly reminded Chico, cost money. They could barely afford to feed themselves.

And it's not like Peanut was the cute and cuddly type. Nah, according to everybody in the neighborhood, including Chico, Peanut was the craziest-looking animal they'd ever laid eyes on.

First off, he took the term "mutt" to a whole other level. He was a mix of ten, maybe fifteen, different breeds. Everything from pit bull to poodle. He was knee-high, with long, spindly legs, an oversized head, and teeth so buck and crooked he could hardly close his mouth. Chico's friend Marco swore Peanut was too ugly to be a hundred percent dog.

"Is it me," he once asked with a serious face, "or does that mutt got some kind of reptile thing going on?"

"It's them bulging eyes, bro," Danny Muñoz agreed. "Look how far apart they are. Like a lizard."

"At the same time," Marco said, "he sort of got this wolf thing happening, too. Don't he look like a wolf, D?"

"His dad was probably a wolf," Danny

said. "And his moms was an alligator. He invented a new breed, man. A wolfigator."

He and Danny Muñoz touched fists, and everybody laughed and laughed and laughed. Except Peanut, who stared up at the three of them with his tongue going, oblivious to the bad-mouthing, happy to just be hanging out.

Peanut was old, too.

Chico assumed he had arthritis 'cause every morning it took him almost a full minute to get to his feet. Chico's grandma swore he'd once had a nice, shiny brown coat. But now Peanut was a poofy purple-gray, like old-lady hair. Except on the top of his head, where he was balding like a man.

And Peanut had a terrible problem with gas. He'd sound off all through the night.

But it wasn't the sound that killed Chico. It was the toxic smell. Some mornings, he'd wake up literally suffocating.

Chico's old man tried tying a small air freshener to Peanut's collar, but the gas smell was too powerful. Chico had to hold his breath whenever he sat down to pet his dog. And even then his eyes would still burn.

None of it mattered, though.

To Chico, Peanut was the greatest dog a kid could ever ask for. In fact, Peanut was more than just a dog. He was family.

That's why Chico swore he'd never stop looking.

He'd tape a handwritten sign to every lamppost in America if that's what it took.

Peanut Situation Goes from Bad to Worse

Soon as Chico got home from school, on the day of the fight, he tossed his bag on the couch and canvassed the neighborhood again, calling Peanut's name, knocking on doors, taping his flyers to any flat surface he saw.

But still.

There was no sign of his dog.

When he finally made his way back home, he found his old man in his usual spot. In front of the TV, dirty work boots kicked up on the coffee table, watching his favorite show, *Cops*, and drinking a beer.

"Yo, Pop," Chico said, "you got any idea what happened to Peanut? I looked everywhere."

His old man shrugged, continued working a toothpick in his teeth.

"It's been two whole days," Chico said. "I don't know what I should do."

His old man just sat there, never took his eyes off the drunk trucker getting patted down on TV. When he finally spoke, he told Chico in Spanish, "Your school called."

Chico froze.

"Said you got in some trouble. That right?"

It was Chico's turn to shrug.

He'd been hoping his old man would avoid this call, like he avoided just about every call from outsiders, by pretending he didn't understand English.

"A fight, Chico?" His dad stood up, snatched Chico by the chin, and looked over the scrapes and bruises on his face. He shook his head. "They told me next time you're gonna be suspended. That happens, you know what I'm gonna do, right, Chico?"

"What?"

"Kick your skinny butt myself. Then send you back to Tijuana to live with your Auntie Mariposa. How's that sound, Muhammad Ali?"

Chico didn't say anything.

When his old man turned back to the TV, shaking his head, Chico went to his tiny room and threw himself onto the futon bed.

He pulled down the two pictures he had pinned to his corkboard. The first was him and his mom. Weeks before she passed. Chico was little, barely a kid yet. His mom had a tiny smile on her face, but her eyes were made out of pain. The mini version of Chico in the picture was oblivious to this pain. He was caught in the camera's flash laughing. Like a clown.

The second picture was him and Peanut.

Taken a few months ago by Marco, outside the greenhouses. Chico's hand on his dog's balding head. Bucktoothed Peanut gazing up at Chico like he was the greatest.

Like Chico would always protect him.

Except he hadn't.

Chico thought back to the day the picture was taken, how after Marco went home, Chico sang the national anthem in Peanut's ear. It was their silly ritual. He didn't even remember how it started. Whenever Chico went after the high notes, Peanut would howl at the moon, like he was singing, too. Both of them so off-key Chico imagined windows shattering all around the neighborhood.

Chico lay there on his futon bed, staring at these two photos, one after the other, thinking of his mom and his grandma and his howling dog and the fight at school and his greenhouse friends and his old man's boots on the coffee table. He felt so confused it was like he was lifting out of his own body. Like he was float-ing up toward his bedroom ceiling, looking down at himself. Who was this lonely kid lying on this unmade futon bed? Holding these worn photos in his greasy fingers?

He snapped back to reality when he realized his old man was standing at his door, watching him.

Chico sat up.

His dad took a swig from his can of beer, wiped his mouth with the back of his hand. "Listen, boy," he said.

Chico was listening.

"Nobody walked that dog."

"What?"

"Nobody fed that dog. Nobody filled them holes that got dug up."

Chico looked at his old man, standing in his doorway, gripping a can of beer.

Then it hit him, what his old man was saying.

He choked on his own breath.

His dad took another swig, walked away shaking his head.

The next morning, Chico worked up the

courage to ask directly. Just before his old man got to the front door, he said, "Yo, Pop."

His dad looked over his shoulder.

"You took Peanut somewhere?"

"Had to," he said.

Like a punch in Chico's gut. "Where? The pound?"

His old man shook his head, switched his lunch box from one hand to the other.

"Where, then?"

"A ranch in Fallbrook, about fifty miles from here. He'll be better off, Chico. He's with a bunch of other dogs just like him."

"But he liked it *here*."

His dad shrugged. "Now he can dig all the holes he wants."

After his old man went out the front door, Chico sat on the couch and looked at his feet. He couldn't move. He imagined arthritic Peanut trying to stand on a ranch somewhere in Fallbrook, sniffing for someone familiar, someone who might sing the national anthem in his ear.

David Winters's Girlfriend

Days later, Chico was at his desk during lunch.

He'd stopped going out on the lawn with everybody 'cause it was awkward sitting alone. Plus, he could just as easily eat in the classroom. His teacher didn't care. And this way he didn't have to fight the glare from the sun reflecting off whatever page he was reading in his book.

Today, though, Chico wasn't reading.

He was staring at one of the flyers he'd made for his lost dog. Before he knew his dog wasn't actually lost but given away.

"Excuse me," he heard a girl voice say behind him. "You're Chico, right?"

Chico spun around.

Meagan Marshall, David Winters's girlfriend. She was wearing a black sweatshirt with the school emblem and a short denim skirt. Her long blond hair was so shiny and pretty up close it didn't seem real.

"Listen," she told him, "I'm sorry about what happened with you and David the other day. How he called you 'compadre' and all that." She smiled, added, "Even though technically you did throw the first punch."

Chico looked at Meagan. He couldn't think of anything to say, so he nodded.

"Anyways," she said. Then she looked down at his lost-dog flyer, asked, "Is Peanut your dog or something?"

Chico covered the flyer with his notebook.

"You lost him?"

"Sort of."

She frowned. "How do you sort of lose your dog?"

"My old man," Chico said. "He gave him away to a ranch."

"Why?"

"So he could dig all the holes he wants."

Meagan cringed.

Even with her face scrunched up, Chico thought, Meagan was still prettier than ninety percent of the girls at school.

"Do you have a picture?"

"A picture?" he said.

"Of your dog, Peanut."

"I think so."

"You're not very definitive with your answers, are you?"

Chico shrugged. He decided the pre SAT was ten times easier than talking to a pretty girl like Meagan.

"Bring one tomorrow," she said. "I wanna see what a dog named Peanut looks like."

Chico watched her gather her hair in a ponytail, wrap her black band around it, and pull it through.

"Anyways," she said again. "I just came in

here to apologize on David's behalf. Even though technically you started it."

"Okay," Chico heard himself say.

Meagan smiled and walked out of the classroom.

A Peanutless Existence

Over the next couple weeks, Chico kept seeing dogs.

Everywhere he went.

Boxers and terriers and pugs and golden retrievers and plain old mutts like Peanut. They were running wild near the greenhouses, stalking through the parking lot at the mall, they were on billboards advertising life insurance, on leashes at the park, they were sticking their heads out of passing trucks, chasing squirrels over fences and birds into trees.

Chico would sit and watch them and think of Peanut.

Once he tried humming the national anthem to himself, but he didn't even get to the high part. It wasn't the same.

Chico boycotted his old man for a while. Whenever the guy came home from work, Chico would get up and go to his room. Even when he didn't have any homework.

But the dad ban only lasted a few days.

One night he came into Chico's room while Chico was studying.

"What's going down?" he said in Spanish.

Chico lifted his chemistry textbook without turning around.

"Need help?" his old man asked.

Chico shook him off, but the dude sat down anyway, took the book out of Chico's hands, and started flipping through pages, nodding.

"It's about chemicals," he said.

Chico shrugged.

"Even water's made of chemicals," he said. "You know that, right, boy? It's called molecules. They all get attracted together with magnetism, and that's what makes the tap water you drink."

Chico stared at his old man.

The guy had no idea what he was talking about.

"Most people don't know that," his dad added, running a finger over the periodic table.

Chico studied him: sitting on the edge of his son's futon bed, flipping through the pages of a chemistry textbook he couldn't read, fingernails caked in dirt, shirt sweat-stained and worn thin from hard work.

An odd thought struck Chico.

Maybe his old man was lonely, too.

Chico cleared his throat, said, "Even tap water, Pop?"

"That's right, boy," his dad said, looking up. "Plants and animals, too. Everything in the world. It's all made up of things people can't even see."

Chico nodded.

His dad smiled, said, "See, boy? Your old man maybe works with flowers all day, but he gots a little knowledge, too."

"I know it, Pop."

He tossed the textbook back onto Chico's lap and stood up. Pointed at the book, then tapped his temple. "You remind me of your mom, Chico. She always liked to learn about stuff, too."

"She did?"

His old man nodded. "It's a good way to be."

Chico watched him walk out of his tiny room, knowing he could no longer be mad.

The Picture

Chico continued dining in at school. Table for one. Sometimes Meagan would pop her head in and ask if he brought the picture of Peanut. And even though it'd be burning a hole in his back pocket, Chico would tell her he forgot.

Two weeks after their initial meeting, though, Meagan walked all the way into Chico's classroom while he was studying and sat in the chair next to him.

She looked at him, said, "Well?"

"What?" he said.

"You bring the picture?"

Chico looked at his desk.

"Lemme guess," she said. "You forgot. Again."

Without really thinking about it, Chico pulled the picture of Peanut from his back pocket and laid it on the desk.

Meagan picked it up.

She covered her mouth and said, "Oh. My. God."

"I know," Chico said. "He looks kind of weird."

Meagan looked up at Chico and laughed. Then apologized.

She studied the photo again, said, "Is it me, or . . . ?"

"What?"

"Or does he sort of look like a wolf?"

Chico couldn't help himself. He cracked a smile.

"Right?"

"My friends say that he's part wolf and part alligator."

They both laughed.

Chico was slipping the photo back into his pocket when he heard a guy voice at the door. "Hey, Meagan."

It was Gabe. "We're going to the library," he said.

"The library?" Meagan said. "You guys?"

Gabe shrugged. "Baker won't give us an extension on that Civil War essay."

Gabe looked at Chico and then looked back at Meagan. "Anyways, Dave wanted me to tell you."

"Cool, meet you guys there in a few."

Gabe was already leaving when Meagan called out, "Gabe, wait!"

He popped his head back into the classroom.

"This is Chico," she said. "Chico, this is Gabe."

They both mumbled, "Hey."

Chico closed his textbook, and Gabe looked at Meagan and said, "We'll be in there."

And that was the end of it. Gabe left.

"See?" Meagan said. "They're not such bad guys."

Chico shrugged.

"Anyway, sorry I laughed at your dog. It's just his teeth. They, like, really stick out."

"I know."

"Like, far, though. I wonder if my mom would ever work on a dog. She's an ortho-dontist."

Meagan patted Chico's shoulder, got up, and grabbed her book bag. She gave Chico a little wave and walked out of the classroom.

The Wolf

A couple mornings later, there was a big rumor spreading around campus. A wolf was loose on the school grounds. Several groups of kids had spotted it on the field before first bell rang.

School security was out in full force, riding around the field on their carts, check-ing inside storage rooms, behind the hand-ball walls, up the hill. Principal Van Buren was walking through the halls gripping an electric megaphone.

Chico's first-period teacher, Mrs. Blizzard, explained how the private school had been built right up against the woods, where wolves still bred. Now that developers were pushing in on both sides, the wolves' natural habitat was getting squeezed.

"Doesn't surprise me at all," she said, closing her roll book and leaning against her desk. "Of course they were going to end up on campus eventually. They're looking for food."

A girl across the room from Chico, Sarah Knowles, raised her hand and asked, "Would a wolf hurt people?"

"Best to err on the side of caution," Mrs. Blizzard said, looking out the window. "That's why they're keeping us inside until Animal Control arrives."

More hands went up, but before anybody was called on, the phone rang.

Mrs. Blizzard picked it up, and everybody

around Chico turned to one another and started talking about the wolf and whether or not they'd cancel school.

Chico was barely listening, though. He kept going back and forth on the thought stuck in his head. A wolf? Really? Or what if it was just a dog that looked like a wolf? Of course, Fallbrook was over fifty miles away. And there was the whole arthritis thing. But still. Imagine if it was Peanut!

The teacher hung up, shouted, "Class, please! Quiet down!"

The hum of conversation faded, and they all turned their attention back to the front of the room.

"That was Secretary Mulligan. Animal Control has arrived. Everything should be fine in a couple of hours. Now, please take out your readers and turn to page forty-seven."

The class groaned and started pulling out their books.

A few minutes into Mrs. Blizzard's lecture, Chico raised his hand and asked if he could use the bathroom.

"I don't know, Chico. They'd really like us to remain in the classrooms."

"It's an emergency, though," Chico said. "I'll hurry."

The teacher looked at her watch, then out the window. "The bathroom and back," she said. "Got it? No dillydallying."

Chico hustled out the door.

Instead of ducking into the bathroom two doors down from his class, he sped past it toward the field. He spotted a few men in safari-looking uniforms wandering around with walkie-talkies and a large net. The school security guards were right alongside them. Principal Van Buren was pointing up at the woods.

When everybody started toward the other end of campus, Chico snuck down onto the field and began a search of his own. He circled the new baseball diamond, ducked in and out of both dugouts. He walked the outside of the track. He marched up a bank covered in ice-plant flowers, peeked behind the rows of portable classrooms.

But there was no sign of any wild animal.

Chico was about to head back to class when he decided to check one last spot. Along the concrete wall just off campus, where he waited alone every morning for school to start.

Halfway up the stairs, he heard breathing.

Chico froze.

What if he was wrong? What if it really was an actual wolf? And it was looking for food?

He stood perfectly still for several long seconds, trying to decide what to do. His heart pounded inside his chest. On the other side of the field, he could make out the people from Animal Control and the security guards. They were leaning a tall ladder against the gym, which separated the east side of campus from the woods.

As Chico turned back around, he saw the shadow of a large animal head slowly peeking out from behind the wall.

His body went cold.

But then he smelled the horrible gas.

And he saw the crooked teeth.

Chico raced up the rest of the stairs as Peanut started patting his feet and moving his bald head around in excitement.

Chico slid to his knees and hugged Peanut, and Peanut licked his face and jumped up so his paws were on Chico's thighs.

Peanut smelled even worse than usual, but Chico didn't care. He rubbed his face all over Peanut's face. Hot dog breath in his ear. Sandpaper tongue. It was a miracle he had his best friend back.

He pulled away and looked at Peanut, said, "How'd you even get here, boy? I thought you had arthritis."

Peanut panted.

Chico's eyes burned.

He imagined the old dog limping along the sides of roads for over fifty miles, somehow finding his way here, to Chico's private school on the hill.

He leaned into his dog's ear and hummed

a portion of the national anthem. Peanut howled into the cloudless sky.

As Chico hugged his dog again, even tighter this time, he felt a couple tears sneak down his cheeks. He wanted to believe they were purely tears of joy, but he knew better. The toxic smell was also a factor.

Ditching School

Chico stood up, knowing he had a decision to make.

If he went to Animal Control, they might ship Peanut back to Fallbrook. He could leave school right now and walk Peanut home, but technically that would be ditching. His old man would flip when he got the call, maybe even ship him off to Tijuana. But could Chico really trust a hole-digging dog to stay hidden behind a wall until the end of school? There was no way he could let Animal Control snatch Peanut up.

Chico guided his dog back behind the wall and said, "Stay, boy."

They stared at each other.

"You hear me?"

Peanut panted, faded tongue bobbing over his buck teeth.

"I'm serious," Chico said. "Just for a minute. Don't come out."

Then he took off down the stairs, across the field, and up to the office, where he asked permission to go home. He was really sick, he explained to Secretary Mulligan. Maybe some kind of stomach flu. He was probably contagious.

But the secretary said they couldn't release sick students without a ride home. Especially with the wolf scare. "You're welcome to lie down in the nurse's office, though," she said. "And I can call home, see if your mother or father can come get you."

Chico considered this.

His dad wasn't near a phone. So that was out. And if he left without a ride, he might end up at Auntie Mariposa's in Mexico. But how could he just leave his dog sitting behind a wall all day? Even if he stayed put, Animal Control would eventually head in that direction. They'd catch him in their special net and take him away. Maybe to the pound. And what would the people at the pound do with a dog as old as Peanut? Put him to sleep?

"Honey?" the secretary said.

Chico looked at her, said, "I'll just wait in class, ma'am. I think my stomach's feeling better."

Meagan stopped Chico on his way back through the hall.

"Hey," she said, hanging halfway out of her classroom door.

"Hey," he said.

"Where you going? We're all supposed to be in our classrooms, you know."

Chico shrugged.

She tilted her head a little. "What's wrong?"

He whispered in her ear. "It's my dog. He came back."

"Peanut?" Meagan shouted. "Where? When?"

Chico put his finger to his lips for her to lower her voice. "Here," he whispered. "By the big concrete wall right off campus. Peanut's the wolf."

Gabe stepped out from behind Meagan, said, "What's going on?"

"Chico's dog," Meagan said in a quieter voice. "The one I told you guys about. He came all the way here from Fallbrook."

Gabe looked up at Chico. "He walked? That's, like, fifty miles."

"Exactly," Meagan said.

Gabe reached into the classroom and pulled another body toward the door. It was David Winters. "This guy's dog," Gabe explained, "traveled fifty miles to find him."

"Are you serious?" David said.

Chico nodded.

"You're taking him home, right?" Meagan said. "No way your dad could refuse a dog that walked fifty miles to find its owner."

Gabe opened his mouth like he was gonna say something, but right then the bell rang. The teacher inside the classroom shouted, "Only go from room to room, people! Field's off-limits!"

Meagan, Gabe, and David stepped out of the classroom. A few other people moved past them, headed toward other rooms.

"They told me I can't leave," Chico said.

"What do you mean you can't leave?" Meagan said.

"Secretary Mulligan. She told me I have to have a ride. Otherwise it's ditching."

David looked at Gabe and then looked back at Chico. "Let's go get your dog," he said.

Everybody turned to David.

"He came all this way," he said. "It's, like, special circumstances or something."

"Dave's right," Gabe said.

Meagan had a big smile on her face. She peeked into the class at her teacher, then turned to Chico and said, "Let's go."

The three of them were now looking to

him. Wanting to help. Chico could not believe it.

He started toward the field, and they followed.

At the top of the stairs they all stood staring at Peanut.

"Wow," Gabe said. "I've never seen a dog with a receding hairline."

Meagan laughed and said, "I told you guys."

Peanut went on his hind legs out of excitement, but as he did this, a very loud sound came from his backside.

David crinkled up his nose and turned to Chico. "Dude, did your dog just rip one?"

"He does that sometimes," Chico said.

Everybody shielded their noses with their hands. "Oh my God," Gabe said. "That's the worst thing I've ever smelled."

When the laughing died down, David patted Chico on the shoulder and said, "Lead the way, man. If you're getting in trouble for ditching, we're all getting in trouble."

"We're in this together," Meagan said.

"You sure?" Chico said. "It's on the other side of the freeway. Behind Home Depot."

"Near the flower fields?" Meagan said.

Chico nodded.

"We don't care," David said.

Chico tried to hide his smile as he took Peanut by the collar and they started walking.

"Does your dad work the flower fields?" Gabe said.

Chico nodded. "You know those poinsettias at school? Near the library?"

They said they did.

"My dad raised 'em up from tiny little seeds. Like a pea in the palm of your hand."

Everybody seemed impressed.

As they passed underneath the freeway, into Chico's side of town, he imagined how they must've looked moving down the middle of the rundown street. Chico leading his crazy-looking mutt by the collar. An arthritic wolf-dog that had somehow tracked him down from fifty miles away. Three white kids from the school on the hill. Escorting him.

Kids he'd fought with on the field less than three weeks ago.

He knew when his dad got home he'd have some explaining to do. He'd have to make a case for keeping Peanut. And he'd have to face whatever punishment his dad laid down for ditching school.

But they were gonna be okay, Chico decided.

All three of them.

Peanut and his dad and Chico.

Something about making new friends made him believe this.

Brancusi & Me

Written and illustrated
by Jon J Muth

Polaire

An Outing

Did you hear that!? It's not a chop. It's a crack! That is splintering of wood! And now comes the bad language. . . . "*#$@&!" Brancusi's voice. Yes! That means we will be going out! That's the third adze handle he's broken this morning. A walk! A walk! He has no more oak! We have to go to Old Man Berg's for ax handles!

Again, the voice, "Polaire! Get your shoes and coat!"

"Ha ha! Yes, you are so funny!" I bark. Brancusi says these things to amuse himself. He knows, of course, I am a dog and don't wear shoes. "Woof! I am ready! Ready ready ready! I am by the door! Let's go!" I say. This is wonderful! So many rare smells! We will pass through the park at exactly the right time. The second baguettes of the day will be baked, and children will be there!

We return home from our outing. That was magnificent! I shall be full for at least five minutes.

I love to hear him muttering under his breath. "The essence . . . not feathers, not a bird, but the essence. . . . What is the essence of a bird . . . ? Not to transcend the animal, but to reveal it more fully!"

I am lying on the concrete floor. He is standing with a stone file, creating a white fog of dust as he smoothes the marble.

"Master," I bark, "no one knows what you are talking about! What does this mean?! The 'essence'?"

"Flight!" he bellows. "Of course! It's flight!"

I can't help it, my tail is wagging/dusting the floor.

"Not the bird . . . but . . . *flight itself*!"

He looks down at me, pulls thoughtfully at his beard, then turns back to his work with the file.

I lick the bottom of his stool leg and watch as fine white particles catch the sunlight. Sometimes, when he is working feverishly, it gets so heavy, I can see sworls in the light.

When they sometimes turn into angels, I am up and barking. You must be vigilant with artists. You never know what their work will bring forth.

Woof! The dust has me sneezing again. I put my paws over my nose to try and stop it.

He laughs at this. He has a sweet laugh.

"Polaire! You are sneezing at my hard work." He crinkles up his eyes, and they sparkle from beneath his brows like a secret hidden in a dark forest. That's when I smell it: love. Even through the marble dust I can smell it. I can always smell it. And that makes my heart leap and fills every corner of the world.

If I'm lucky, that's when he comes in close and snuzzles me—his Romanian word—and no matter how much he washes, I can still smell the wood smoke in his beard. Smells like home. And the marble dust. Always the marble dust. My nose may not be able to smell as well as when I was a puppy, because

of the dust, but my ears are very good, and so are my eyes. I can see many things in the stone and many things in the wood. I try not to bark because it breaks his concentration. Then he puts me outside. The door is always open, but I know he would rather I stay outside if I am going to bark.

Sigh. There is much less to talk about outside. Rue de Ronsin has so little traffic. Crazy automobile drivers sometimes. Maybe one of Giacometti's cats will saunter by on a good day, and that can be a nice chase. Of course, I let Brancusi know when visitors are coming. Especially Duchamp. He always brings small sausages for me. Duchamp should come more often.

We enjoy Erik Satie's company very much these days. The music he and Brancusi play together is such fun: Satie playing that crazy old piano from the Russian painter in the next alley and Brancusi on a flute he carved himself.

Satie will come by the studio and play bits for Brancusi, sometimes working at the stunted piano all afternoon. Satie has been writing this sonata for a while, which he describes as a prayer. It has tender, sad passages and crashing desperate themes freely mingled, one after the other so splendidly, so powerfully, so naturally that it is no longer the sounds of music that fill the studio rooms, but the flow of Satie's memory, heard now for the first time. Satie's whole being seems to pour into this piece of music.

"Constantin"—this is Brancusi's given name, and Satie insists on using it—"I finally have a well-paying commission. It is for an opera. It is to be in the key of A and will revolve around the theme of a fairy tale. Anyone could write it. I am barely involved," says Satie. "The whole thing is outlined. Just a lot of labor, signifying nothing. But it is a big affair." The older pianist polishes his pince-nez glasses and plops them back on his nose. "Costumes, sets, so much time fiddling with this or that part because the soloist can't reach a note. Anyone could write it," he says, without a trace of pleasure in his voice. "And so I will spend the next year or more trying to help get this cement albatross off the ground."

Brancusi looks at his friend for a moment. He has been working on his magic bird—his *Maiastra*. "I have to remove a shadow from the neck of the *Maiastra*," he says. "It is important that a certain line stand out in relief." His eyes are watery. "A billion possible lines pass through a point, and I must choose from a billion lines . . . one . . . single line. No one knows where that line is but me. If I don't find it, it will never be found."

I look from Satie's face to Brancusi. In all Brancusi does there is a gentleness. Even carving the largest of stones there is an insistence of faith in the goodness of things. As his work progresses, he will stand face-to-face with some potential that only he can yet see. And when the work is finished and his sculpture stands in the room, the potential that he saw, now revealed to be the *one*—will be more real than all the others.

Satie looks at the younger Brancusi, who is focused intently on his seemingly perfect and finished sculpture.

For a long time that evening, when we are alone, a fire in the hand-built stove, Brancusi sits in a chair near my bed of woodchips just patting my head and thinking.

"Satie's music," he mumbles. "It's like a river flowing to all of his feelings. He is almost incapable of keeping it inside. That opera may lock it away. Satie is capable of showing us ourselves, what it is like to be here, alive, right now. But this opera will take much effort, and bring forth . . ."

Brancusi looks at me very seriously. "Polaire, what becomes of an artist when the necessities of the world drive him sane?"

The next day Satie visits. He brings biscuits. He has dropped the commission and will continue to work on his own music.

This is the effect Brancusi has on artists.

The Portrait

Brancusi is looking at me seriously. His sculpture of the magic bird—*Maiastra*—is behind him, framed against the bright window. It is too intense. I have to look away. He paces this way and stops. He paces that way and stops, never looking away from me. I show him my good side.

"What?! Master, what?!" I yip.

"Polaire," he says, "chisels cost money."

I sneak a look at him.

"Axes, saw blades, hammers, all cost money." He starts to walk around the room, rubbing his beard, woolgathering. "Not to mention food," he says.

"It's okay, mention food," I woof.

"True," he says, gesturing around the studio, "I can make most of the tools. . . ."

"And the food," I think.

"And I have made all of the furniture we need."

It's absolutely true, I think, looking at the large plaster table and the wooden stools and that comfy pile of woodchips.

Brancusi sits down heavily, as if he has been sentenced to the gallows. "We could use some money, so I am going to do a portrait bust," he says.

I'm not sure why, but I lay my head down in sympathy. I feel as if someone should come and tie a black veil over my head.

"Portraits are so difficult," he says sadly, looking at his shoes. "A portrait is an invitation to failure for an artist."

"Yes," I think. I put my head in his lap. "It is . . . wait, why?"

"We can never love the subject in the way the person asking us to do the portrait would want. If we are very lucky, we will succeed on the lowest level—it will *resemble* the subject." He says the word *resemble* like it tastes bad. His thick fingers stroke my white fur. "If we attempt the impossible, if we try to find a universal beauty underlying the distractions of outer appearance, if we try to capture some timeless essence, we will not be understood."

"Maybe you should stop complaining. Just do the bust, and see what happens," I think.

He looks at me. Marble dust flecks his eyebrows. His tiny eyes sparkle in a smile.

So the lady from Paris comes to our studio. . . .

I try to make her feel welcome once I realize she hasn't brought a bizarre and lazy animal with her. She is wearing a fur coat. She is a strange woman. I think she worries she is being followed. She keeps looking into all the mirrors. I want to tell her that I once barked at mirrors because I too thought something was there. Of course I was a pup then. She is a full-grown woman and should know by now there is nothing in a mirror!

My Brancusi is very charming, and in a few minutes, she is laughing and very comfortable. When she doesn't accept my offer of the bed of wood chips, I decide enough is enough, and I take my afternoon nap.

Weeks later, when Brancusi finishes the bust, even I am surprised. He has captured all that

strangeness in just three beautiful, simple shapes.

Saturday night is when we have visitors. I am near the fireplace helping to lick up the splashes of a very tasty stew, called *gulyás*, which Brancusi kindly sloshed over as he stirred the pot. There is a sharp rap on the door, and Marcel Duchamp's face appears.

"Maurice!"—this is what Brancusi calls all his most pure-hearted friends—"You have been away too long! How was America?"

"Excellent! And full of interest in your work," says Duchamp.

I lick the final delicious *gulyás* droplets as Duchamp gives Brancusi a great hug. "Look who is joining us this evening!" he says. Then Duchamp, with a lovely smell of sausages, waves around his elegant new walking stick. Erik Satie and a friend of his who is a poet step inside the studio, followed by some young dancers and a painter. The mirror lady is there. She is very happy. The Russian painter who gave us the piano and his little girl. She is very shy. I do my best not to look at her right away. They all enter and take their favorite places. More and more people seep in, giving the all-white cathedral-like space intimacy and warmth.

Duchamp holds his new cane up. "You must admire my new *whacking stick*!" he says with a funny American accent.

"I think you mean *walking* stick," says a guest with a slightly better accent.

Duchamp raises the stick, "No, no! Here, lean this way. I will demonstrate!"

I see the little girl cover her eyes with her hands, and I bark for the grown-ups to stop.

Can't they see they are frightening her?

Satie sits down at the piano.

Soon Brancusi has the little girl dancing with him and everyone is laughing. When the dance has ended and her shyness returns, I gently pluck a warm roll from the cutting board and give it to her. We spend the rest of the evening curled up together under the table, fast friends, dozing off now and then. That's how these evenings are.

And then, dawn at the windows; the night has gone. Most guests have left; stragglers are sleeping on couches and divans. I've finished eating the sausages and, sadly, most of Duchamp's coat pocket. Staying up late could be a bad habit. It clouds the senses.

The sun is rosy across the rooftops. I can hear the hotel on the boulevard waking up, the windows opening, flowers being set out, everywhere fresh scents, coffee, newspaper boys calling out the morning headlines.

My Brancusi is, on the other hand, working on his magic bird, his *Maiastra*. He stayed up all night after the guests had either left or fallen asleep, and I can see he is very tired. He steps back from the marble and sighs. For many minutes, he doesn't move. I hear someone snoring. Then Brancusi notices that

Duchamp has left his beautiful new wooden stick. He loves working in wood. It's a joyous material for him, I can see that. When I was a puppy I would chew the heavy scrap pieces. I think wood reminds him of when he was young. All the houses where he grew up were carved from wood. I've heard him tell this again and again to whoever will listen.

Then he looks at me with a grin and slips the walking stick behind his back. For a moment, he is young and mischievous. I think I see a young Brancusi's foxlike cunning. A few hours later, I hear the sounds of a flute from the carving room.

The Beginning of the World

Today he lifts a white dustcover and it softly falls away from a great long, graceful piece of marble like a fin, resting on its knifelike edge. I sit and look at the shape, hypnotized. Brancusi pushes gently on one end and it spins slowly round. It is so big and yet so thin it almost disappears as it turns.

"When you see a fish, you do not think of its fins and eyes and scales, do you?" His bright little eyes are twinkling. "You think of its speed, its floating, flashing body seen through water!"

He sits down on the bench next to me and scratches behind my left ear. We look at the fish slowly spinning; its surface catches the light and flashes like polished silver as it turns.

"I want to express just that," he says. "If I made eyes and fins and scales, I would trap the fish in a pattern or a shape of reality. I want just the flash of its spirit."